Von Richthofen and Brown

A mud-slathered German infantryman, his battalion dug in a few hundred yards west of the aerodrome, stood in the trench holding a newspaper in his hand and gazing over the parapet at the planes taking off one by one. A photograph on the front page showed Richthofen and his grinning comrades in front of their newly painted planes: RICHTHOFEN'S FLYING CIRCUS PLAYS IN ARENA OF DEATH. WESTERN FRONT AWED BY ACES.

'There goes Voss,' said the infantryman. 'And now Wolff . . .'

Other soldiers were watching too, and one of them took up the litany.
'Hermann Goering . . . and Udet . . . And –'

'There he is! That's Richthofen himself!'

And they watched the blood-red Albatros D-V climb into the sky, envying him and the other pilots their clean, beautiful, noble style of war. While on the opposite side of No Man's Land, hundreds of British infantrymen were gazing upward as the Hawker Squadron droned overhead, and thinking the same thoughts.

Von Richthofen and Brown

Joe Lavinia

TANDEM
14 Gloucester Road, London SW7

Originally published in the United States by Universal
Publishing & Distributing Corporation, 1971
Published in Great Britain by Universal-Tandem Publishing
Co. Ltd, 1971

Made and printed in Great Britain by
Hunt Barnard Printing Ltd., Aylesbury, Bucks.

Germany, 1932

Max Holzapfel puffed calmly on his pipe and waited for the next customer. The moth-eaten booths of the little traveling carnival were almost empty, now that it was starting to rain. It was a soft rain, like a mist, but it made customers scarce.

Across the cobblestone square stood an old beer hall with the door wide open. Holzapfel could see part of the crowd inside, sitting on benches, listening to a male chorus singing a rousing military song. He tried not to listen. He had had enough of war.

Two figures approached. Clearly they were father and son. Inside the beer hall the singing stopped abruptly, and an expectant hush settled over the crowd. The man and boy stepped up to Holzapfel. He nodded pleasantly to them both, pretending not to notice that the man was wearing the Brownshirt uniform with swastika armband. The Nazi stared arrogantly at the older man through thick glasses.

"You are the operator of this particular ride?"

Holzapfel nodded yes, puffing his pipe.

The Brownshirt leaned down toward his son. "Willi, this is what you wanted? Eh?"

The boy was feasting his eyes on the pint-sized World War I plane models, just big enough for a boy his size to ride in. He dashed from plane to plane, each one swaying gently in the moist breeze. The one on the end was a Fokker DR-1 Triplane replica. It was painted bright red.

"This one, Poppa. I want to ride this one."

"Very good, Willi—give the man your money."

Dutifully the boy reached out and put a coin in Holzapfel's hand.

"I must go now," said the Brownshirt. "I'm already late. You'll be good, won't you? Eh?" He turned to Holzapfel. "Operator, the boy will continue to ride while I attend to business across the street. Will you keep an eye on him?"

Holzapfel nodded coldly. He was familiar with this type of man. The new German patriot! Bah!

The Brownshirt strutted off toward the beer hall. At that moment a strident voice rang out harshly from inside the building. The principle speaker, Herr Adolf Hitler, was commencing his address. The voice seemed to reach out and fill the square with its ugly vibrations. Holzapfel had heard it before, on the radio. He had not wanted to hear it again.

Holzapfel helped the boy ino the plane. The boy's smile was almost beatific.

"This is the best one, isn't it?"

Holzapfel nodded and began to pull the control lever. "Some thought it was the best of them all," he said.

There was a faraway note in his voice now, a note of regret, as he thought back into the distant past.

The ride creaked slowly to life and began to swing the little planes like a merry-go-round, to the music of a Viennese waltz of chimes, and the boy became giddy with excitement.

But the chimes did not drown out the sound of the strident voice from inside the hall. It didn't matter to Holzapfel. He was back in the past now, recalling the most glorious days of his life, the days when he was associated with his country's most brilliant warrior. His eyes were on the boy, watching him clutch the imitation gun-control in one hand and the steering column in the other, probably pretending he was Richtofen; but Holzapfel was thinking of a man who didn't need to pretend anything—Baron Manfred von Richtofen himself . . .

Chapter 1

Baron Manfred von Richtofen was peering over the side of the cockpit of his old Albatros C-III, watching something far below in the snow-covered Russian landscape. At first it was only a tiny dot at the edge of the forest, but as he steered his obsolete scout-craft in that direction it took form and shaped itself into a beautiful bull elk, already stirring nervously at the drone of the engine.

Pressing the stick forward, Richtofen swooped low and lined up the animal in his sights; then, bending his rudder a fraction, he let loose a three-bullet burst of machine gun fire and saw a puff of powdered snow appear beside the elk. The animal started with a massive shudder, and within two seconds was running at full speed across the white and frozen land. Richtofen, grinning from ear to ear, his eyes glinting with hunter's glee, had time for two more short bursts, one on either flank of the madly galloping beast, before he roared on by and upward into the blue—and on the final burst Manfred von Richtofen nearly killed himself.

He had been very close to the ground when he pressed the trigger the last time and saw the puffs of snow at the elk's heels. Suddenly, his body was jolted as the landing gear bounced off the frozen earth; for a split second, Richtofen's right hand was off the stick and the plane was veering and coming down off its bounce toward an obliterating crash. At the last moment, as the elk vanished into the forest, Richtofen delicately regained control with the touch of mastery that made him the instinctual pilot he was, and the Albatros righted itself and climbed to safety.

Richtofen was covered with cold sweat.

For several minutes, as he flew homeward, he fumed at his clumsiness. It was the clumsiness more than the brush with death that offended him. He was grateful that none of his comrades had seen it.

There was one more moment of clumsiness to endure before his flight was over. As he touched down on the air strip, flashing past the hangars and the row of planes, the tip of his left wing dipped because of the damaged landing gear. It began to scrape with a loud tearing sound and, starting to dig in, caused the entire plane to do a soft ground loop. When the dust had cleared, and all was quiet, the Albatros was standing on its nose.

Max Holzapfel was the first crewman to reach the plane, and there was a look of panic on his face. But Richtofen was already climbing out of his safety belt and had one leg over the side. He was smiling, but Holzapfel could also see that he was embarrassed.

"A slight miscalculation, Holzapfel. The smallest kind of error. Nothing really."

The crewman, trying to keep a straight face, helped him climb down. The two men stood staring at the

plane and its broken wing, as the rest of the ground
crew ran up to them, aghast.

A hundred yards away, on a railroad siding just
beyond the last hangar, stood a lone coach that served
as the squadron's bar. Sumptuously decorated in the
Edwardian style, it was a veritable palace car, with a
billiard table, dining table, and several comfortable club
chairs. Two officers were playing billiards, and others
either watched the game or sat in the chairs reading.
Almost everyone had a glass in his hand or on a table
beside him.

Apart from the rest sat two majors, looking out at
the landing strip. One of them, the one with the *Pour
Le Merite* medal around his neck, was the premiere ace
of the entire German Air Corps. His name was Oswald
Boelcke, and he had just arrived on the Eastern Front.
No one yet knew the exact purpose of his visit.

Boelcke was watching Richtofen cross the field,
heading toward the coach. When the young baron entered at the far end, the veteran flier turned in his chair
and watched him walk up to the men playing billiards.
The first player had just completed a carom, and was
shifting into position for the next shot.

"It's simple logistics, you see," commented the other
player, a sarcastic smirk on his face. "If you don't
make this shot, I'll never trust you with a machine
gun."

Richtofen plucked a cigar from a nearby humidor
and lit up. The officer was taking a long time to make
his shot. When he finally struck with his cue, the result
was a miss. Amid the shouts of disparagement, Richtofen coolly reached out for the cue, his hand poised in

the air. He did not look at the player, but merely waited for the cue, cigar clenched between his teeth. Somewhat reluctantly the man pressed the long wooden rod into Richtofen's hand, and the young flier proceeded to put on a show of animal grace and skilled calculation that drew the attention of everyone in the coach. Richtofen shifted with an absolute minimum of movement from position to position, leaning over and squinting in coiled silence before each shot, making one point after another.

"Nice," said the player who had handed over the cue. "You're getting a style, Richtofen."

"No," said the young Prussian. "I *have* a style."

Over by the window, Major Oswald Boelcke gestured toward Richtofen with a tiny glass of brandy. "What about him? The one playing now."

The other major shrugged. "You wouldn't be interested in him."

"Oh?"

"He's the one you just watched make that ridiculous landing."

"Even so," said Boelcke, "he seems to have—"

"—he seems to have a certain incapacity with aircraft," the other man cut in sardonically, and it occurred to the visitor from the Western Front that his companion had had his share of the brandy. "He failed his flight training twice, and almost failed the third time."

"You mean he requires more training," said Boelcke, as mildly as he could.

"I mean he's a menace to life and property," said the major loudly. Then, in softer tones, he grumbled, "He's some corn-fed Silesian nobility, *minor* nobility. Name's Richtofen. *Von* Richtofen, if you please."

"Have you nothing good to say for him?" asked Boelcke, a twinkle in his brown eyes.

"Well . . ." the other allowed grudgingly, "he does have a certain instinct."

Richtofen was poised over another shot. A moment of concentration and then, with an economy of movement that did not escape Boelcke's sharp observation, the plunging cue drove the ball around the table; with a neat succession of clicks Richtofen made point.

"Are you planning to grant me an inning, Richtofen?" inquired the player from whom he had taken the stick.

"The game is taking, Lieutenant—not giving." And Richtofen continued moving around the table like a hunter stalking game.

There was no question in Major Boelcke's mind by now that this young officer was a natural competitor, with a special ingredient highly prized by the air ace at the moment—ruthlessness. He rose from his chair as Richtofen completed his final shot and lay the pool cue on the green baize of the table. Standing upright for the first time since he began playing, Richtofen puffed on his cigar, removed it from his mouth, looked at it with an air of amused self-satisfaction, and stuck it back between his teeth where it jutted out at a jaunty angle.

"Gentlemen," said the over-brandied major in a formal voice, "allow me to present Major Oswald Boelcke."

The visitor from the Western Front stood facing von Richtofen, and could not fail to observe that the big cigar was now drooping; obviously, the young officer was very impressed.

"You're . . . Oswald Boelcke?"

"Yes, Herr Rittmeister," said the older man, smiling engagingly. "Why? Have we met?"

"Yes—I mean no, sir—I *know* you, of course. Everyone knows you. You and Immelmann and the others."

Boelcke was already shaking hands with the rest of the officers, but he continued his conversation with Richtofen. "You keep up with the Western Front, I see."

"We have a great deal of time for reading here."

"Come with me."

"Sir?"

"I said, 'Come with me.' We're going for a stroll."

Meekly, Richtofen followed the older man out the end of the coach. For the first time Richtofen noticed how neat Boelcke's uniform was, in comparison with the officers who were his comrades here in Russia. It was because the war was so dull here, he supposed, that the men lost interest in keeping up appearances. Not that anyone was outright sloppy—yet no one was *immaculate,* as was the visitor from the Western Front now walking beside him, hands clasped behind his back.

"I take it you are not . . . *content* with this assignment."

"Oh, I've never complained," said Richtofen quickly, almost defensively. "The Army is my profession."

"Is it unprofessional to have a preference?"

Richtofen looked over at him and saw the sly grin.

He grinned back. There was something about him that Richtofen liked. The man certainly commanded respect, yet there was nothing in the least intimidating about him.

By now they were standing beside the cowling of one of the scout planes on the flight line. "This isn't just idle curiosity on my part, you know. I'm forming a new squadron."

He stared at Richtofen significantly. Richtofen dropped his cigar to the grass. "You mean—you mean you'd take *me?*"

"I can promise you a chance. It would mean a great deal of work on your part. I saw your . . . landing."

Richtofen was embarrassed for the second time that day. "I don't mind work. I *thrive* on work. That landing, it was—"

"Never mind. We will work on your flying, together."

It was getting dark now. Richtofen wondered how long they had been talking. In silence they strolled back to the coach and stood for a moment in the light streaming out the rear door. Boelcke could sense that Richtofen had one question to ask. He waited in silence.

"But—"

"Yes, Herr Rittmeister?"

"But why *me?*"

Boelcke laughed. "I liked the way you play billiards."

Richtofen stared at him and then offered a tentative smile. Boelcke could see that he didn't understand. But there were no further questions along that line. Stand-

ing there in the light, with the darkness of the Russian
night on all sides, Boelcke saw that, in spite of his
confident manner, Manfred von Richtofen was a very
young man.

He won't be young for long, Boelcke thought with
regret. *When I get through with him, no one will ever
call him young again.*

Turning, he climbed the three steps and went inside.

Chapter 2

Two days later, Boelcke and Richtofen were flying over occupied France, the veteran leading the way in a Pfaltz, the newcomer at the controls of a two-seater scout plane. Riding in the second set, in front of the pilot, was a very nervous Max Holzapfel.

Why couldn't he have let me come by troop train? Holzapfel grumbled to himself. In his heart, he knew that Boelcke was going to challenge the young pilot to some sort of display of skill before they landed at the new base—probably to show him how much he had to learn. Holzapfel waited miserably for it to start.

Up ahead, Major Boelcke turned around in his seat with a smile on his face . . .

Here it comes, thought Holzapfel.

. . . and suddenly the Pfaltz slipped gracefully into a double barrel-roll. Holzapfel slowly reached out and gripped both sides of the cockpit in a death grip. Behind him, Richtofen smiled tolerantly, then bit his lip in concentration and jerked the control stick back between his knees. The plane lurched upward, stalled, and fell off clumsily. In a moment it had righted itself and Holzapfel allowed himself to open his eyes. Richtofen

was furious with himself once again for clumsiness. He
would have to do better next time.

Next time was *now,* for Boelcke was already banking
the Pfaltz into a power dive. It was done smoothly,
beautifully. Richtofen watched him pull out of the dive
thousands of feet below . . . and then he noticed that
Holzapfel was staring at him over his shoulder, trying
to get his attention. Richtofen nearly laughed in his
face—the crewman looked so furious. But the meaning
was clear enough, as Holzapfel repeatedly jabbed his
finger toward the top wing, shaking his head over and
over.

Richtofen chose to ignore him and, pushing the stick
forward as smoothly as he could, brought the old scout
plane into a dive. Holzapfel closed his eyes tightly and
tried to pretend he was somewhere else. Below him, the
earth seemed to rise up to swallow the little machine,
and Richtofen began to feel terror himself as the motor's roar filled his ears, the wind pressed his cheeks,
and the plane itself began to vibrate alarmingly. In a
few seconds he had reached the limit of prudence and
safety; now he would go a few seconds more, to show
Oswald Boelcke what manner of man he was. When he
pulled out, a hundred feet from the hard earth, the
terrific strain on the top wing pulled a strut loose and
the breaking wire made a sharp cracking sound like a
rifle shot. For one fleeting second, Richtofen experi-
enced a terror he never knew existed. But the wing
stuck, the plane leveled off, and for the second time in
a week he found himself cold with sweat.

Richtofen pushed back his goggles, his face transfigured with a brilliant smile of joy and youth and pow-

er. He had flirted outrageously with death, but death had not seduced him. Throwing back his head, he roared with laughter, but the wind and the motor obscured it. Major Boelcke steered his Pfaltz to a parallel course and the two pilots looked at each other. Richtofen found it impossible to wipe the grin off his face as the veteran stared over at him. Richtofen imagined he could discern a look of frank admiration in Boelcke's eyes, even though they were twenty yards apart.

As soon as Richtofen touched down on the runway, his frazzled passenger began clawing his way out of the cockpit, where he had been prisoner ever since they took off from the field in Russia. He jumped to the ground and stood shaking his head and reaming out both ears, as Richtofen slowly climbed down. Before the trembling crewman could open his mouth, to let out the torrent of complaint and recrimination he had stored up, the young pilot put his hand on Holzapfel's shoulder.

"You were fine up there, Max. Really fine. There may be a decoration—"

It took a moment before Holzapfel understood that he was being teased, but then he burst into loud laughter and Richtofen joined him. The laughter was perhaps a little louder than was called for, in their common realization that they had moved through the valley of the shadow of death together.

Boelcke walked up to them and Richtofen greeted him with a huge smile.

"I congratulate you, Herr Rittmeister. You obviously have—"

"—more skill than you thought?"

"—more luck than you deserve."

The smile faded from Richtofen's face.

Boelcke beckoned him over to the plane, just behind the left wings. He reached up with both gloved hands and gave a single hard push.

The entire top wing came loose with a crack, tipped forward, and came to rest against the engine cowling. Holzapfel covered his face with his hands, all the terror back in his heart. Richtofen merely shook his head in astonishment.

And then he threw his head back and laughed, and Holzapfel glanced over and began to laugh too. Their laughter carried an unmistakable tinge of hysteria as they roared on and on. Boelcke stood there patiently.

A sharp voice interrupted the scene. "Is *this* what you brought back from Russia, sir?"

The two men stopped laughing.

There were several young officers standing behind Boelcke, pilots every one. The man who had spoken was a stocky, sarcastic-looking fellow who stood there eying Richtofen with a disapproving air. His name was Hermann Goering.

"You should have packed him in straw and sent him in a barrel," said Goering.

Boelcke quickly stepped in with introductions. "Gentlemen, this is Baron Manfred von Richtofen—"

"*Baron?*" said Goering, his eyes widening in mock reverence. He turned to share his amusement with a dark scowling fellow beside him.

"Herr Rittmeister," Boelcke continued, "here we have Lieutenants Hermann Goering and Ernst Udet. I introduce them together because that is how one usually finds them—on the ground or in the air."

One by one Richtofen shook hands with every man present, conscious that they were his comrades-in-arms, that they were men he would perhaps grow closer to than any other humans on the face of the earth—if he survived long enough.

Breaking up into two groups, they strolled back toward the operations shack and Richtofen had a chance to look around him. It was immediately apparent that this aerodrome was in much finer condition than the one in Russia. He saw an unusually large number of crewmen, all wearing amazingly clean overalls. He noticed the neatly painted hangars, barracks, and operations shack, and the care with which the planes had been aligned. Beyond the field lay the ruins of a French village and beyond that, as far as the eye could see, a blasted and desolate landscape where nature had been virtually neutralized by a months-long rain of artillery shells. The aerodrome sat like an oasis of green and brown in the midst of sterility.

"And have you gentlemen completed your training?" Richtofen politely asked the men walking beside him.

Lieutenant Werner Voss smiled and shook his head. "No one is finished training here. Major Boelcke says we'll never be finished. There are no masters in the craft of air warfare. Not yet. It's too young, too new."

Goering, walking on the other side, shook his head in disagreement. "It isn't a craft, Voss. It's an art. Training never made a master. You have to have . . ." He groped for the right word. "You have to have the *instinct*."

Richtofen nodded, knowing that what the pudgy fellow said was true. Voss leaned over and muttered in his ear. "He's a hell of a flier. If anyone has the instinct, he does."

Goering heard him and smirked wolfishly.

"The only thing he cares about, though," Voss continued, in a louder voice, "are women and—and paintings."

Goering turned visibly red in the face. "Not quite all," he said. "Just wait until this war is over . . ."

"Oh yes, I forgot," said Voss, snapping his fingers. "After the war, Hermann is going to be a very big man."

Ignoring this sally, Goering took his leave with a slight nod of his large head and stalked off.

Up ahead, the pilot named Kurt Wolff was walking beside Boelcke. Richtofen cocked an ear to get the drift of their conversation.

"Things have gotten hotter since you left, Major," Wolff was saying. "The British have a new scout plane with a Lewis gun mounted on the wing, and a Vickers firing through the propeller."

Boelcke nodded ruefully. "So they have the interrupter-gear, do they? I suspected they were on the verge. It's hard to stay ahead!"

Plodding along behind them, Manfred von Richtofen fairly vibrated with anticipation, yearning almost sensuously to climb up into the exclusive battlefield of the sky and show the British—interrupter-gear or no interrupter-gear—the kind of pilot he was.

Now that he had proven himself to Boelcke, perhaps the major would let him go up that very day to begin a career he knew was going to be illustrous, if not outright glorious.

He decided to ask him.

Richtofen went up that day all right, and the next day too, and several more times after that—but not to meet the enemy. Boelcke knew that his young hero was far from ready. The two of them worked together in the clouds, Boelcke showing him all the tricks he knew about handling a plane, and little by little the young baron acquired a solid grasp of the techniques of maneuvering a plane in combat-like situations.

On the ground, between flight-training sessions, Boelcke held formal classes in the operations shack, standing before a blackboard while his star pupil took notes.

"Aerial combat is a chess game minus the board," Boelcke said, during one of these classes. "The machine gun on your plane is nothing. Anyone can pull a trigger. It is *position* that counts. Position is everything. When you have an enemy plane in your sights at one hundred yards, the rest is simple. But to *get* him there, you see—that is the trick."

And so, hour after hour, the two of them practiced the most complicated patterns in the clouds, until at last both planes moved almost as one, their timing so coordinated that, to observers below, it seemed as if they were tied to a single string.

In class, one day, Boelcke said that in combat there is no time to think, which seemed to Richtofen almost a ludicrous remark—but he had grown to trust his teacher implicitly.

"You look doubtful, Herr Rittmeister. You will learn that thinking is useless. You have only to *react*. What you do will become a part of your nerves, your muscles. You will become a complex device, and feel the machine become a part of you like a second skin that answers your will as readily as your own hand does."

And still there was more flying to do. Richtofen was having trouble controlling his impatience. One afternoon, as soon as they had rolled to a halt on the landing strip, he jumped out and stalked over to Boelcke, who was just unstrapping his safety belt.

"Major, I am ready."

Boelcke looked at him with a kindly expression on his face, seeing how intensely anxious the young flyer was.

"Soon," he said. "Very soon now."

That very afternoon, Boelcke put Richtofen through his final tests. As the sun began to slant low in the west, Richtofen found himself standing with a double-barreled shotgun in one hand, a shell in the other. Ten yards to his left front, Major Boelcke stood with a trapshooting device for hurling clay pigeons into the air.

"Are you ready?" asked Boelcke.

"But why am I doing this? None of the others—"

"Did you think I brought you all the way from Russia to do what the others do?"

"But I can fly well now. I can do anything—"

"What you can do, I can teach anyone to do. I want to see what *else* you can do."

And with a sudden surge of movement he threw the

clay pigeon into the air and waited until its long arc began curving back towards the ground.

"Now!"

Richtofen whirled, loading as he went, threw the shotgun to his shoulder and fired. The clay pigeon fell to earth untouched.

"Once more, Herr Rittmeister."

Boelcke casually reloaded the trap and sent a second target through the air, the sun's golden rays catching it vividly against the late-afternoon sky.

"Now!"

This time the clay pigeon was blasted to powder. Richtofen turned to his teacher for approval, but Boelcke said only: "I think we'll try one more batch."

With that he signaled to a ground crewman who, unbeknownst to Richtofen, had been standing in the background the whole time. The man brought forward a large black container that looked like a suitcase, but wasn't.

"Get ready," Boelcke ordered the young flyer. Richtofen took out another shotgun shell and stood ready to load and fire, his gaze skyward. Boelcke took an object from the crewman's hands and immediately hurled it into the air.

"Now!"

Richtofen loaded and fired, and saw a live pigeon vanish in a puff of feathers.

"Excellent," said Boelcke. "You no longer think, you react."

"Well, what about it, Major? Now?"

Boelcke stared at him for a moment. "Yes, Herr Rittmeister. Now."

Chapter 3

Boelcke's enemy counterpart, the commander of the nearest British squadron, was a man named Lanoe Hawker. Hawker was an old-fashioned gentleman. His men, who worshipped him, knew him to be not only brave—all officers were expected to be that—but kind and compassionate as well, unusual characteristics in an outstanding warrior. Lanoe Hawker had vowed at the beginning of his career to do his fighting by "the rules of war" which meant adherence to fair play and the avoidance of brutal behavior. He expected his men to do the same. There were many men like Hawker at the beginning of the war in 1914, but when the armistice bells tolled across Europe four years later most of them were dead and the rest had different values.

The first time Manfred von Richtofen accompanied Major Boelcke's squadron on an actual combat patrol, he watched Hawker shoot down one of the baron's new-found comrades, a youngster named Engler, and in his mind's eye he could see the hated Englishman leering evilly as the shattered German plane spun around and around in a corkscrew dive to earth. In reality Lanoe Hawker's expression was one of profound sadness as he watched Engler plummet to oblivion. But to Richtofen all Englishmen were "hated Englishmen." At this point in his career, the war was a relatively simple affair: kill Englishmen, then turn around and kill more Englishmen—and Frenchmen too, if they crossed your sights.

In this first combat mission, Richtofen had tangled briefly but harmlessly with Hawker, and that was the sum of his day's fighting. Little as it was, it left him trembling with excitement. Holding back on the periphery of the dogfighting, as Boelcke had strictly ordered, he had suddenly found the opportunity to send a burst of machine-gun fire at a British plane that swooped in front of him momentarily. His aim had been true: Three tiny holes appeared in the canvas of Hawker's Spad, right across the target-like British insignia to the rear of the pilot. But then Engler had engaged Hawker and that was the end of it for Richtofen—and, in a more profound sense, for Engler.

For all his bravado, Richtofen was shocked to his depths by his comrade's fall. He was getting his first lesson in war. Soon enough the calluses would be hard on his soul, and he would watch men die with absolutely no reaction whatever. And then, still later, those calluses would begin to dissolve and the pain would begin. But that was a long time in the future.

When Lanoe Hawker and his men came within sight of their aerodrome, the thing that first caught their eyes, as always, were the shining whites the cricket players wore on the field adjacent to the landing field. It never failed to amuse Hawker to see this tiny bit of

England in the midst of a shell-scarred landscape. The cricketeers themselves, pilots all, paused in their game to count the planes, matching them against the number they knew should be coming back.

The number did not match. It rarely did.

Wing Commander Willard Owen had not counted the planes, but when he walked up to Hawker, he could tell by the man's face that there were some who would never return from the mission. Hawker had just climbed down from his Spad and was peeling off his flying suit. The depth of his sorrow was written with painful clarity on his face.

"How many . . . ?" asked Wing Commander Owen.

"Too many. Too damned many."

"Easy, Lanoe. It's not your fault."

"No? Then *whose?* I send men up in kites to meet the finest planes and best pilots the German Empire can put in the air. Every time we take off it's virtually a suicide mission."

Hawker tossed the leather suit over his shoulder and the two men walked toward Operations. The Union Jack snapped in the light breeze on the flagpole in front of the building. The breeze also carried across the shouts of the cricketeers, and their competitive noises only plunged Hawker deeper in gloom.

"This morning I had breakfast with Chub Rodgers," he said. "Twenty minutes ago I saw his plane fall apart with one of Boelcke's people pounding him to pieces, like a hawk on a helpless robin."

"I was at breakfast too," said Owen. "And I was the one who ordered the mission."

Hawker nodded numbly.

Parked near the building was a Sopwith Camel with two men working on it, and something about them caught Wing Commander Owen's eye. He walked over to them, Hawker following. A Royal Canadian Air Force officer's jacket hung from one of the wings, and the owner, a young fellow in shirtsleeves, sleeves rolled up, had his arms deep within the engine cowling. An older man, a mechanic in overalls, stood close by.

"It's ... about six inches long," the young officer was saying. "There's a connecting rod, and some sort of ... bolt."

"Right you are, sir," said the mechanic. "That's it. Now, if it's loose, just give it a half-turn. Fell into place, right?"

"Now, do I use the spanner—or what?"

"Right—you've got it, sir."

Wing Commander Owen stepped forward now. "Well, what have we here?"

The young officer turned around, stared, then broke into a clumsy salute which left a glob of grease on his forehead. Lanoe Hawker was amused enough by the man's clumsiness that he forgot his broodings over the losses he had suffered. This young man, whoever he was, was a replacement for the dead and there as some small cheer in that.

"Lieutenant Roy Brown, sir" said the young man, identifying himself.

"Brown?" said Owen. "Of course. I received your orders yesterday. Lieutenant, this is my executive officer, Major Hawker."

Brown reached out to shake hands but, seeing the

grease on his own hand, drew it back. Hawker reached
out and took the hand anyway, ignoring the grease.

"Very good to know you, Lieutenant. I see you're
interested in engines."

"Back home there was farm machinery. I used to fix
it, so I—"

"Of course," said Owen, and he turned to the
mechanic. "You'll finish up for the Lieutenant, won't
you?"

"Certainly, sir."

Owen and Hawker were strolling toward Operations,
with Lieutenant Brown between them, wiping his hands
on a handkerchief, his uniform jacket tucked under his
arm.

"You've been a combat pilot before, haven't you,
Brown?" Owen was asking.

"Yes sir."

"And how would you assess the competition?"

"Competition, sir?"

"The Jerries."

"I think they're a pack of butchering sons of bitches,
sir."

Owen and Hawker exchanged surprised glances.
Hawker cleared his throat in embarrassment. His own
pain at British losses in the air had never actually fixed
upon the German Air Force in terms of *butchery*. The
choice of words seemed excessive to Hawker, gentleman that he was, but he replied in mild tones: "I
suppose our opposite numbers over there feel their
losses as badly as we . . ."

"Undoubtedly," said Owen, somewhat at a loss for
words himself.

Brown raised his head and looked at each of them in turn, looked at them oddly, as if there was something strange about them. They seemed to be taking the Germans' side, almost. Roy Brown was not a complex person, and his emotions were keyed to the obvious. And the obvious was that the Germans were a pack of butchering sons of bitches. It was obvious to Roy Brown, former Canadian farmboy, that if you had an enemy, there was only one way to regard him—with unrestrained hatred. Especially when that enemy's dearest wish was to take your life.

Chapter 4

Another German combat patrol was about to take to the air. Major Oswald Boelcke was making what was to be his final statement to his pilots.

"We must hit them harder, gentlemen. We have the better equipment at the moment, but our advantage cannot last forever. We must win while we have it." And then, his voice rising sharply, he shouted, "Man your planes, and good luck to you all!"

The pilots ran to their planes and climbed into the cockpits. As Manfred von Richtofen settled down in his Albatros D-III, Max Holzapfel leaned over and strapped him in.

"He wasn't speaking to you alone, Herr Rittmeister," said the ground crewman, by way of gentle warning. "You are not expected to win the war single-handed."

Baron Richtofen smiled grandly down at him, as the crewman climbed back to the grass. "Are you sure, Holzapfel? Why not? I may give it a try."

The engine, already running, only awaited Richtofen's touch on the throttle. He applied the pressure suddenly, and the plane moved forward with a jump that nearly knocked Holzapfel down.

A few minutes later, the squadron was passing over the Cambrai battlefield, an expanse of land that resembled the landscape of the moon. Hundreds of muddy and miserable infantrymen huddled below in trenches and dugouts, and a few of them glanced upward at the droning formation of German planes far above the filthy, deadly world they knew.

Richtofen was the one who spotted the British reconnaisance plane, flying close to the ground, heading toward the German lines, and not far behind, the Hawker squadron. It was an awesome sight, and the young baron was momentarily stunned by it—the sight of so many enemy planes so vulnerable, so unsuspecting. But then the fierce, sensual urge to attack overcame him and he waved to Major Boelcke, waved frantically to catch his attention. When he succeeded, he jabbed his thumb downward over the edge of the cockpit, indicating the enemy's position.

Boelcke went into action with a rapidity that startled the younger man. After waggling the wings of his plane, he simply peeled off into a long straight swoop toward the enemy formation. Richtofen and the others peeled off behind him and now the squadron was descending like screaming eagles.

Lanoe Hawker saw them at the last possible moment and tried to signal to the others. Lieutenant Brown, reacting fast, looped into a violent barrel-roll just as a German plane loomed ominously behind him, guns blazing—and the German found that he had tangled with the wrong man. Brown stubbornly bent his angle of barrel-roll until the German's escape was pinched off. A streak of tracers arrowed out from Brown's machine guns, pinioning the German craft in midair and the pilot as well. There was no smoke, there was no destruction visible to Brown's peering eyes, but the German pilot had been destroyed by a single flaming tracer round through the chest. His plane began rolling softly toward the earth.

Brown did not have time to relish his kill, for almost immediately another German plane was locked onto his tail and he launched into a series of would-be evasive maneuvers that failed to evade. Although he didn't know it, his relentless pursuer was the German air force's greatest ace, Oswald Boelcke.

A hundred yards above their tight duel, Lanoe Hawker happened to glance down and see them, and knew at once that Roy Brown was in over his head. With a kick of his rudder he veered downward and hove to behind Boelcke.

As this drama was quickly unfolding, Richtofen was stitching the brown fabric of a British two-seater and watching the wood fragments of the frame and bits of canvas come flying back toward him in the enemy's slipstream. Abruptly the British plane exploded and Richtofen's craft was showered with fragments, part of his windshield blown away. The young baron, momentarily disoriented, wiped his goggles and looked around . . .

And saw his teacher and master in trouble, and gasped.

Lieutenant Goering saw it too, and, reacting like an airborne cat, sent a stream of tracers into Hawker's plane.

Hawker veered off, escaping.

Boelcke, avoiding a collision with the onrushing Richtofen, veered upward—and was unable, barely, to avoid touching Goering's landing gear with the tip of his wing as he passed overhead.

To the rapt infantrymen below it seemed harmless enough, but a second later another British plane attacked Boelcke with a burst of bullets. When Boelcke bent the machine into its initial evasive turn one of his struts came spanging loose and then another; and then, as hundreds of men watched below in fascination, and Richtofen and Goering in horror, the top wing crumpled fluttering in the cold air.

In the unstable, vibrating plane, Oswald Boelcke knew his number was up. He had been expecting it to happen, sooner or later. A man can't watch his comrades-in-arms die all around him week after week and be surprised when Death at last points his bony finger at him. Some hidden impulse made Boelcke unstrap himself and climb out onto the wing. The plane was not yet entirely out of control and—yes, that was it— he wanted to meet Death on his own terms, not hitting the earth inextricably trapped in the midst of a whirling piece of useless machinery.

Goering and Richtofen were flying on either side of the fluttering plane, both men feeling agonizingly impotent as they watched Boelcke.

Boelcke looked over at Richtofen for a moment. Then he gave a short wave that the young baron thought was the most impressive gesture he had ever seen.

"Goodbye, sir," said Richtofen, the wind drowning the sound.

Boelcke released his hold and began his final journey, tumbling over and over as the plane began to break into pieces. It was a nightmarish sight that was to haunt von Richtofen for the rest of his life.

Chapter 5

Captain Helmut von Hoeppner was riding in the back of an open Mercedes-Benz with a worried elderly colonel and a very nervous major. The colonel, a relic of the Franco-Prussian War and proud possessor of a dueling scar on one cheek, was worried because he had been told to resolve the "Boelcke problem." Or was it the "Richtofen problem?" The major was very nervous because the road leading to the aerodrome was filled with shell holes, and yet the corporal who was driving seemed to think the Mercedes was a plane, and he was trying his best to make it fly. Captain von Hoeppner was, as usual, utterly serene. He was too busy figuring out a solution to the colonel's problem to bother about the possibility of going into the ditch.

"I say it's a mess, any way we choose to deal with it," the colonel was saying.

"Don't you think it would be wise," suggested the captain, "to minimize that element of the problem, sir?"

"Eh?"

"Boelcke is dead, and he was, shall we say, *impor-*

tant? They say the Emperor himself followed Boelcke's exploits."

"Well, then?"

"The question—it seems to me—is what to *do* about it."

The very nervous major was unable to stand it. "Corporal," he shouted, "slow this car down. And for God's sake try to avoid at least some of the—"

The car lurched violently and the major was thrown back into the seat. He opened his mouth to shout again, but von Hoeppner cut him off.

"I beg your pardon, Major, but I understand this section of the highway is under observation by French artillery spotters."

"I don't care if it's *mined*." He turned on the driver again. "Corporal, slow down. Slow *down*!"

There was an onrushing sound like a giant freight train, and an artillery shell exploded a hundred yards up ahead, leaving a rolling bank of black oily smoke. The major, chastened, sank back into the cushions.

"This fellow Richtofen," said the colonel.

"It's *von* Richtofen, sir. Silesia, I believe."

"If this Richtofen did indeed cause the unfortunate accident, I suppose we're expected to—to nail his carcass to the tree?"

Von Heoppner, noting the colonel's tentative plea for advice on the matter, smoothly came across with his solution. "I don't think we need a martyr for this situation, Colonel."

"You don't."

"Not really, sir. If the colonel likes . . ."

The elderly man glanced over at von Hoeppner. "What is it the colonel is supposed to like?"

"I may have an idea. Something that would solve—"

The sound of a motor, which no one had noticed until then, expanded swiftly to a roar. A British plane was following them down the road, its machine guns flickering. Before any of the four men had even turned around to look, a line of holes appeared in the windshield.

"Damn you, Corporal," the terrified major screamed, "give us top speed, do you hear? Do you want to die? Give us more speed!"

Captan von Heoppner, seeing the plane overfly them and continue on, with no sign of a second strafing run, looked at the white-faced major with quiet contempt. Then he leaned across the man's lap and picked up the conversation where he'd left it, offering the solution to the Boelcke problem to the colonel.

And the colonel listened.

Lieutenant Hermann Goering was livid with rage, stomping up and down beside his plane as the other pilots watched.

"Stupidity, do you hear? Not courage or cleverness— just stupidity. Boelcke is dead because—" and here Goering nearly choked on his own rage "—because a damned clown from the provinces was greedy for another glorious victory."

Richtofen was standing alone and apart, ten yards away, standing stiff and drained of color, listening, taking the lash of Goering's words against him.

"It was *your* landing gear Boelcke hit against."

Goering whirled around to see who had spoken. It was Kurt Wolff. "You're the one he hit," Wolff continued. "Why didn't *you* pull up, eh? Boelcke didn't hit Richtofen, he hit *you*."

Goering stood rooted to the spot, stunned by this unexpected attack by one of his own comrades. He glared at Richtofen. "So that's it. My God, if only I had a *von* in front of my name. Then my comrades would stand behind me. No, on second thought you're all peasants. You align yourselves with the baron of the castle here, as if you were serfs."

Richtofen had had enough of this venom. Slowly he moved forward to face the stocky lieutenant, his seething emotions barely under control. "I did what I thought was best. The Englishman—I felt that if I could head straight into him, as if to ram him, he'd ..." But the words choked off and the young flyer gestured helplessly, imploringly. "I owed Major Boelcke everything. If I could have taken his place, believe me—"

Goering, pretending to misunderstand his words, turned grandly to the others. "Did you hear that?" He flared back at Richtofen. "You'll never take his place—you, the very one who killed him." Goering gazed skyward melodramatically and spread his arms. "Oh God, if they ever give me this squadron—"

"I'll put in for transfer ten minutes later," said Kurt Wolff. Goering lowered his arms slowly and looked at Wolff and then at the others. Their eyes were cold. He would get no support from them, that was certain.

Richtofen had a faraway look in his blue eyes now, as if he hadn't been listening to the argument around him. Richtofen was seeing ghosts. Ghosts of the mind.

Oswald Boelcke had come back to haunt him.

There he was! Falling toward earth, as before, tumbling over and over.

If Wing Commander Owen had a German counterpart, it had to be Major Franz Cargonico of the Imperial Air Service. Cargonico was presently trapped behind his desk, a captive audience to the elderly colonel.

"The press, the public," he was saying, "and the Kaiser's own representatives—they all want another Boelcke, Major. And he must be from Boelcke's own squadron."

"I perfectly understand, sir."

"Well, who is it to be, then?"

Cargonico gave a little laugh and shrugged apologetically. "What can I tell you, sir? They're all capable, all brave, but—another Boelcke? That is asking a great deal, if I may be permitted to say so."

"Enough of this," said the nervous major. "The colonel asked you which one."

But Cargonico was not about to be pushed into making a hasty decision he might later come to regret. "Wolff, Voss, Goering," he said evasively, "they're first-rate pilots."

"Fine for the provinces," said the old colonel, "but we need a man for Berlin."

"I—I don't quite grasp your meaning, Colonel."

"The Kaiser wants a fellow with dash, and color—can't you understand me, man?"

It was Helmut von Hoeppner's moment to say the right thing at the right time, something he was skilled at doing. "May I interrupt to ask Major Cargonico a question, sir?"

"Proceed."

Hoeppner looked across the desk at Cargonico. "Who would Boelcke himself have chosen to take over?"

Major Cargonico relaxed, almost laughing with relief. The decision had been made for him. "That's easy," he said.

Baron Manfred von Richtofen stood at attention in the square of the ruined French village, clutching a small ceremonial pillow before him, with Oswald Boelcke's decorations pinned on its purple velvet face. Behind him, the pilots and staff members and crewmen were arrayed in a company formation, with the elderly colonel, the major and the always serene Hoeppner at one side. The coffin itself rested on a two-wheeled, horse drawn caisson. Richtofen's place was beside it, five steps to its left.

It was an hour before sunset, and Boelcke's funeral ceremony was just drawing to a close, with Major Cargonico delivering the eulogy from the edge of the shattered village fountain.

"It is difficult to bid farewell to such a comrade," he was saying. "For me, the task is impossible. I can only speak to you some words which are older than this army, older than this Empire . . .

> *'War is both king of all and father of all, and it has revealed some as gods, others as men; some it has made slaves, others it has made free . . .'*

"I know that if Major Boelcke stood with us today, he would accept this tribute, for it is nothing more than the traditional farewell that German soldiers are wont to pay to their own comrades."

Cargonico's voice quavered to a halt and there was silence. Then Richtofen stepped over to the caisson, moving with measured military precision, and paused there, looking straight ahead. To an unknowing observer he might have seemed like a mindless automaton, fulfilling an official duty, but inside his head the young baron was seething with pride that he had been chosen to carry the dead hero's decorations. He had not yet allowed himself to ask *why* he—rather than Wolff or Goering, or one of the others—had been chosen.

As the sergeant-major barked the order and the drum roll began, Richtofen stepped off slowly, and the solemn funeral march got under way. By ranks, the pilots and staff and crewmen peeled off in the rear of the caisson.

Goering and Udet were marching side by side.

"What's *he* doing up there?" asked Goering out of the side of his mouth. "Why did they give him the decorations?"

"Who knows?" said Udet. "It doesn't mean anything."

Goering, set in his unreasonable hatred of the young baron, muttered, "I wonder what they'd have given him if he'd gotten more of us killed."

Werner Voss, marching ahead in the cortege, shot Goering a disgusted look over his shoulder, as Udet stared ahead, determined to stay above it all.

As the column moved slowly down the road to the

steady beat of the drum, distant echoes of artillery explosions washed over them, and the fear of death that is every soldier's fare reverberated for a moment in their hearts.

That evening in the officers' mess, long after the casket had been put aboard the funeral train, the nervous major was sitting in one of the big leather armchairs, nursing a snifter of brandy. Across from him sat the colonel and von Hoeppner.

"How would you feel," the colonel was asking him, "if you were in his place? Twenty-three years old, about to step into the shoes of a legend?"

"How can I say, Colonel? I was never twenty-three. If I had been, I would have remembered it."

Von Hoeppner and the colonel stared at him, realizing that the man had probably had a touch too much to drink. He was spared further embarrassment, however, for there was a knock on the door.

"Enter!"

In strode Richtofen, glancing nervously around.

"Good evening, von Richtofen," the colonel greeted him. "It's good to see you. Tell me, did I know your father, perhaps?"

"My father?" asked Richtofen, standing somewhat stiffly before them. "It's possible, sir."

Richtofen was standing almost at attention. It was obvious to Hoeppner that the young pilot expected to receive official warning of future proceedings against him in the matter of the midair collision. Why else could he have been summoned? Richtofen was probably asking himself.

But now the colonel gestured toward an empty chair. "Sit down, Richtofen."

"Thank you, sir."

The colonel rubbed his hands together thoughtfully, frowning, as Richtofen waited tensely. "Well, I suppose I should get it over with. This is a difficult moment for us, you understand."

"Yes sir," said Richtofen, not understanding at all.

Hoeppner could barely keep from smiling. Richtofen looked as if he were expecting to be court-martialed on the spot.

"Your record," said the colonel, "and the opinion of those in the squadron ..." He was almost groping for words. He cleared his throat. "It appears that Major Boelcke held you in some esteem."

The major had been fanning himself with the newspaper, just managing to keep his mouth shut, but this was too much. It irritated him, the way the old man was hemming and hawing. "They're going to give you the squadron," he blurted out. "What do you think of *that*?"

As the colonel snapped a look of the utmost dismay at the major, Richtofen half rose from his chair, stunned.

"I think that would be—very nice."

Captain von Hoeppner laughed at the young airman's ingenuousness. He rose and snatched a bottle of brandy and three glasses from a serving table. But there was more to Richtofen's impulsive answer than ingenuousness. It was more a nervous bark than a laugh, for the day's pressure had been hard on him, compounded by his feeling of guilt over his mentor's death, as well as his dread of an official investigation.

But now the colonel, the major and Hoeppner were on their feet, glasses raised. "To Baron Manfred von Richtofen! May he be the leader Boelcke was . . ."

". . . and hunt the British from the skies," added the major dramatically.

". . . and live to tell about it," said Hoeppner quietly.

Richtofen, a son of Prussia to his core, stood trembling with pride and happiness, his young face shining like the sun.

Chapter 6

The next few months flew past like a whirlwind of happy delirium, and one day he awoke to find that he had become a celebrity of the Empire, sought eagerly by interviewers and hostesses and hangers-on. A medal pinned on his tunic by an Austrian general, an invitation to be the guest of honor at the home of an important industrialist—it was all very bemusing, and quite delightful. And in between these "social engagements," as his comrades ironically called them, Baron von Richtofen killed British pilots, destroyed British planes, and gained a mastery of his Albatros that was awesome to Wolff, Voss, Goering, Udet, and all the others.

But his face was no longer the young, eager face of months before. It had taken on a glint-eyed hardness that made him look considerably older than his years. Manfred von Richtofen had never had a highly developed sense of joy, and now his handsome face began to settle into an habitual expression that was almost severe. When he broke into a smile—which was not often—it seemed to cause him a certain effort. The truth of the matter was that Richtofen had become quietly obsessed with killing British pilots and destroying British planes.

"Rittmeister," an obsequious little interviewer was now asking him, notepad poised, "our readers want to know what it's like to fight in the sky."

"If they can pass the examinations, I invite them to come join us and find out for themselves. And now, if you'll excuse me . . ."

"But how *does* it feel," the little man persisted.

"Oh, a bit like waltzing, in a way. Except that your partner is firing a machine gun at you."

"Then, you more or less enjoy all this? The war, and the hunt, and so on?"

Richtofen was on his guard immediately. It wasn't that the interviewer was baiting him, for he was not. How could he guess that Richtofen did indeed love the war, in terms of his own role in it? He was merely asking a rather tactless question, hoping to draw him out. But Richtofen knew that the public would cringe if he exposed his obsession freely. And so he framed a careful answer.

"War is—the father of nations. It makes them slaves, or it makes them free." He tried to recall the rest of Cargonico's quote, but couldn't. Slightly exasperated, he turned to the man and said: "What is a professional soldier *supposed* to feel about war?"

The truth was, he didn't think about it. Manfred von Richtofen was a man of action in the truest sense. He had his duty to perform and that was all there was to it. Why were these people trying to get him to make grandiose statements about a simple duty?

His discomfort over this made him all the more

attractive to his adoring public, who mistook it for modesty.

Richtofen inhabited a room that took up one entire corner of the operations building. At one end of the room was a large window overlooking the flying field, and at the other end was an enormous fireplace with an old wood-framed mantel. Above the mantel hung a big mirror, slanted slightly downward so that a person standing in the middle of the room could see himself full-length. The wall space on either side of it was covered with Richtofen's somewhat grisly momentos of war: bits of wooden propellors, canvas fragments with serial numbers, several of the target-like British insignias, a complete control column, and a Vickers machine gun. The mantel itself was half covered with small sterling silver cups, each commemorating an air victory.

There were twenty-nine of them.

Richtofen stood in the middle of the room, reading a newspaper story about himself in the *Berliner Tagblatt*, and shaking his head in wonderment. It was a strange experience, being a celebrity. The public made you into a kind of god, even though you didn't deserve it. Deserve it or not, Richtofen was having a hell of a good time. He put down the paper and strolled aimlessly around the room, hands in pockets. Then he remembered the package that was resting atop his desk. He picked it up, unwrapped the brown paper and drew out another silver cup. He looked closely at the engraving, which recorded the date of the kill and the type of plane he shot down.

His wintry blue eyes glazed over for a moment as he

conjured up the dogfight for which the cup stood, and into his mind came the awful image of the British pilot's face at the last moment of his life. That face, contorted with hatred and terror, vanished in a sudden splash of blood. Richtofen blotted the horrible image out of his mind, and set the cup atop the mantel along with all the others.

The door burst open and men came shouldering their way in, all boisterous and cheery. Voss, Wolff, Udet, and others came blaring into their leader's privacy, carrying champagne buckets and all sorts of French delicacies in tins and tiny wooden boxes. With a noise that made Richtofen start slightly, Voss eased the cork out of one of the bottles. Richtofen forced himself to smile as Voss and Wolff and Udet approached him, beaming.

"They confirmed the S.E. 5a scout about an hour ago," said Voss. "It almost fell on one of our artillery positions."

Udet spoke up. "That makes you the leading ace of the Central Powers." He coughed into his hand, looking embarrassed. "That is—"

"You don't have to say it, Ernst," said Richtofen. "I know: the leading ace—among the living."

Wolff, pretending to ignore the little exchange, blundered ahead. "You'll be the greatest of them all before it's over."

In the rear, one of the other pilots was describing his last dogfight, complete with gestures and mugging. "Then the bastard went to ground. I had him dead to rights. I waved him down, but he wouldn't have it. He fought like a cornered rat."

And once again, before Richtofen could do anything about it, the ghastly image of the bloody-faced Englishman came vividly into his mind, and he grimaced.

Voss' heavy, hacking cough snapped the baron out of his involuntary reverie of horror. "Lord, this weather," said Voss, wiping his mouth with the back of his hand. "This cold of mine just hangs on and on. No way to get rid of it."

Richtofen studied him with concern. "Werner, the surgeon said you need rest. Do you think I've forgotten? Why are you driving yourself?"

Voss licked his lips and tossed down the champagne, then stared hollowly into Richtofen's eyes. "The same as you: to live my life to the full, while I still have it." Richtofen started to say something, but Voss cut him off with a choppy wave of his hand. "I'm making arrangements for a—a rest. Will you leave it to me, Herr Rittmeister, as to when and how I begin my—my rest?"

And he abruptly launched into a second coughing fit, the door opened and Hermann Goering walked in with a round-faced, friendly looking young fellow who seemed oddly familiar to Richtofen. Goering was lugging a large, flat square object wrapped in burlap, obviously a painting. The batman, who had been dragged along by Wolff and the others to serve drinks and tidbits, now strode over to the two newcomers and put glasses of champagne in their hands.

The young man and Richtofen stared at each other, the young man grinning practically from ear to ear. The baron's mouth dropped open in astonishment.

"Is it *you*, Lothar?"

The young man laughed. "I just came to get your autograph, Oh famous Herr Richtofen."

Richtofen stepped forward and slowly embraced his younger brother, while Lothar concentrated on keeping his drink from spilling.

"Werner!"

"Herr Rittmeister?"

"This is him. This is Lothar, my brother."

Voss reached out to shake the young man's hand. "My God, another one. There'll be no British planes left for the rest of us. You've flown combat before, haven't you?"

Lothar grinned shyly. "A bit, yes. Not as much as any of you, of course."

And cutting ominously into the baron's happy moment came the voice of the same pilot still telling his combat tale across the room. "... but then I got smart. I fired three or four bursts out *ahead* of him—and he ran right into them. My God, to have figured it so closely, I mean, it was—*art*."

Lothar saw his brother shut his eyes tightly, as if to gain control of something in his mind, and realized once again, as he had so often in the past, how different Manfred was in outlook from himself. Lothar was far more fun-loving and outgoing than Manfred; everyone said so as they grew up together. *Manfred is so serious,* he could hear his mother say. Idly he wondered now if that seriousness would make Manfred a better fighter pilot than himself. Out of the generosity of his heart, he supposed that it would. The statistics did not impress him; there was a long war ahead and Lothar planned to catch up to his brother in kills eventually.

One of the pilots was staring at Goering's package. "What the hell is that, Hermann?"

"What, this? Oh, nothing. Nothing at all."

"Come on, Hermann. Don't be a great ass. Is it one of your paintings? Eh? Have you bought another?"

Goering was clearly anxious to show off his acquisition, despite his assumed reluctance. He peeled away the burlap with a flourish, and the men gazed in silence on a landscape painting by Watteau. It was a peaceful, idyllic scene, glowing with a kind of quiet beauty that contrasted sharply in Manfred von Richtofen's mind with the memories of stark violence he had been struggling with for the past few minutes.

"Well?" said Goering. "You like it?"

"It's all right, I suppose—if you like that sort of thing. I'd rather look at a nude painting myself."

"Pah! You have no taste. This is a work of one of the great French masters, and it's worth thirty thousand marks if it's worth a pfennig."

And once more the door swung open, this time to admit von Hoeppner, who in the intervening months had been promoted to major. He crossed the room and shook hands warmly with Richtofen. "My congratulations, Herr Rittmeister, on your thirtieth victory."

"Thank you, sir. Herr Major, may I present my brother, Lieutenant Lothar von Richtofen. And I believe you know Lieutenant Werner Voss."

"Indeed, the personnel of this squadron is becoming well known everywhere," said von Hoeppner smoothly. The batman put a glass of champagne in his hand, and von Hoeppner raised the glass high. "To Rittmeister Richtofen and his squadron. May it continue as it began. And may the Rittmeister's next victory be over Lanoe Hawker himself."

The pilots exploded in raucous laughter, and downed their wine.

Chapter 7

Across the lines, only twenty-seven miles to the west, Major Lanoe Hawker himself proposed a toast later that same day.

". . . To a truly distinguished foe. I give you Baron Manfred von Richtofen."

The other officers in the pilots' mess—all but one—rose and raised their glasses toward the wood-beamed ceiling, said *Richtofen* almost in unison, and downed their wine.

It was the Canadian farmboy who had ignored the ceremony. Roy Brown sat quietly, staring at the checked tablecloth.

"A cultural note, Lieutenant Brown," said an Irish pilot named Gerald Murphy. "There is a certain custom called the toast. It takes place when gentlemen rise and drink in tribute to some object of mutual esteem. It is expected that all gentlemen present take part."

The silence that followed was heavy with the residue of Murphy's sarcasm. The rest of the officers stood poised to hear the Canadian's reply.

Brown glanced up mildly and reached for a roll. He

began to butter it. "I'd rather pass it up, Lieutenant Murphy."

"Is that because you don't care for our wine?"

One of the other pilots, a fellow named Fred Thompson, nudged Murphy and muttered, "He can't drink anyhow, you know."

"And why not?" asked Murphy in a loud voice.

"Bad guts—ulcers. Picked 'em up on his last tour. He—he drinks something *white*."

A pilot named Ridley laughed. "They call that milk, Thompson."

"All right, then," said Murphy, relentlessly pressing the matter, "perhaps you'd rather drink the toast in milk, Mr. Brown."

The Canadian took a bite of his roll and glanced up at Murphy, chewing away. When he had swallowed, he said: "Your Richtofen is not an object of my esteem. And I won't drink to the bastard in wine *or* milk."

In the painful silence that followed, the officers sat down. Brown stuffed the rest of the roll in his mouth. Only Gerald Murphy and Major Hawker remained standing.

"Gentlemen," said the major, "we will let it pass." And turning to look down at Brown, he added: "I'm sorry you feel as you do, Lieutenant, but—"

"You don't own the blighter an explanation, sir! He—"

But Hawker waved Murphy to silence, and the angry Irishman sat down.

"Lieutenant Brown, we believe men can be foes without becoming beasts," Hawker went on. "Those who survive this hell will find they still have need of those traditions that separate gentlemen from savages."

Many of the men nodded respectfully at what Hawker said, but Brown shook his head negatively and pushed the wine glass a little further away from him.

"Major, I say this is no time to admire the antique. I'll save my wine, if you don't mind, for the next gentleman your German knight blasts out of the air."

With that, Brown rose, bowed slightly toward Hawker, glared defiantly at the others, and walked out of the mess hall.

"Graceless bugger!" said Murphy. He beckoned to one of the enlisted-man waiters and pointed to the wine glass in front of Brown's place at the table. "Leave it there, you understand?"

"Yes sir."

"Leave it right there."

"I will, sir."

Richtofen had been sitting in the small hangar office when Max Holzapfel brought him the infuriating order. He read it once and then, rising and striding angrily around the room, had read it a second time.

"What the hell do you mean, *paint* them?" he raged. "How can you conceal an *airplane*?"

Holzapfel shrugged and spread his hands apart in a helpless gesture. "What can I say, Herr Rittmeister? They hand me this paper and . . . and it says to paint—"

"Holzapfel, should a man hide from his enemies?"

"It depends, Herr Rittmeister."

"Should a *gentleman* hide from his enemies?"

The sound of other voices began to reverberate

throughout the hangar, as several pilots approached. Someone was telling a humorous story and the others were making casual sounds of amusement, as they all headed toward the little office.

"Answer me, Holzapfel."

"No, Herr Rittmeister. A gentleman should not hide."

Entering the office, the men immediately sensed the tension, and Werner Voss choked off the story before the punch line. The airmen looked at Richtofen, then at Holzapfel. The crewman silently handed the order to Voss, and the others closed in beside and behind him to read it.

"Son of a bitch, what's this?" asked Voss.

"Paint them?" said Goering with a scowl. "That's stupid."

Mournfully, Max Holzapfel added, "It says to paint them *multicolored* in order to obscure the character and shape of the—"

Richtofen suddenly laughed, interrupting him. "Right! Multicolored. *Now* I have it." And he turned on them with a big wicked grin. "Udet, Goering—go call the crewmen. Turn out the whole lot. Tell them it's special duty. Lothar, you and Holzapfel go to the supply shed and bring me every can of paint you can lay your hands on. And plenty of brushes. If we don't have enough, we'll beg, steal or borrow the rest. Take off!"

The others were already on the run, but Lothar hesitated.

"What colors, exactly?"

"Bring me the rainbow, little brother. Do you hear? I want the rainbow!"

Lothar nodded, looking quite bewildered. He had never seen his brother so exhilarated.

Major Helmut von Hoeppner was addressing a group of civilian newsmen in the operations room, feeling slightly foolish in this unaccustomed public relations role. Major Cargonico stood to one side, beaming politely at the newsmen.

"Germany's bid for a voice in the destiny of Europe is more than a war, gentlemen," Hoeppner was saying. "It's a crusade. And what, I ask you, does that call for?"

"Rationing, Herr Major?" It was a short bald Austrian newsman who had spoken, eying Hoeppner cynically.

"It calls for sacrifice," continued the major unperturbably. "It calls for young leaders who are totally dedicated. It calls for men of blood and iron. You all know of the exploits of Baron von Richtofen and his squadron—"

Meanwhile Richtofen and his squadron, men of blood and iron, had nearly finished directing the harried crewmen in their strange "special duty." Max Holzapfel, standing back to survey the work, moaned, "They're going to send every one of us to the infantry, I know it. They'll have us roasting rats at Verdun."

"Shut up, Holzapfel," said the baron. "Leave everything to me."

The crewman shook his head dolefully and went back to work.

The fighter planes had undergone a radical color transformation. While before they had all been a dun brown, they now gleamed yellow and green and blue. Richtofen stood by himself admiring the sheer garishness of each plane.

Lothar shouted from across the field and the baron turned, and then smiled. His younger brother had managed to requisition a barrel of beer from somewhere, and he and a crewman were rolling it toward the working party. In short order the barrel was de-bunged, drinking steins were rounded up from the messhall, and every man had a beer in one hand, a paintbrush in the other.

Only one plane remained to be painted: Richtofen's Albatros.

"Well, Lothar," he said, rubbing his hands in expectation, "what shall we do with mine?"

"That's up to you."

Richtofen rubbed his chin, considering.

"I think—red. Yes, definitely red."

Lothar laughed at his serious-faced brother, and began to round up the unopened cans of red paint.

Some time later the job was finished, and everyone could see that the baron was having his doubts. Not about the squadron paint job, but about his own plane. It was all red, bright red. Only the black Iron Cross insignia with its white borders broke the solid red coloring.

"Well, Lothar—tell me. Do you think it's too . . ."

"I think it's wonderful. My God, they'll see you twenty miles away!"

At last Richtofen permitted himself a smile, gazing at his transformed Albatros.

Major Cargonico and the newsmen approached the hangar. The major was holding forth in grandiose manner to the visibly bored reporters.

"... he represents the best in Germany today. We want you to meet him, to meet his men, to witness the determination that animates them. Yes, if one embarks on a crusade, *these* are the knights one wants to—"

"—to hire, Herr Major?" It was the little Austrian again.

"You're a cynical man, Herr Richter. Don't you velieve in anything?"

The Austrian merely pursed his lips and looked as if he was about to fall asleep with boredom. The group had reached the hangar, and Cargonico beckoned for two crewmen to pull open the big doors.

"They're just finishing up some work on their aircraft, gentlemen, and they may be a little tired. I hope you'll take that into consideration."

As the great doors parted, the pilots and crewmen inside stopped their feverish painting one by one and stood staring at the newcomers. As before, each man held a brush in one hand, a stein of beer in the other. No one was exactly sober.

Only Lothar carried on with his work, too engrossed to notice the silence around him. "Hurry up, hurry up. We're almost done. Wait till those brass-bound sons of bitches show up! They'll—"

"The sons of bitches have arrived, Lieutenant." Cargonico's hard voice echoed around the inside of the hangar, and the young officer froze, joining the others for a moment in the general freeze. Then slowly turning around, he saw the major and the newsmen, and he looked heavenward as if he were hoping for God's intervention or at the very least an air attack. The rest of the pilots and crewmen watched the baron to see what tack he would take.

"Gentlemen," Richtofen said. "It's a pleasure to see you all."

And the others began to relax a bit.

"Herr Rittmeister," said the major, his teeth nearly clenched together, "perhaps you can explain this to us. I certainly *hope* you can."

"Why yes, Herr Major," said Richtofen, all innocence. "We've been obeying your orders, sir."

"Come, come, Herr Rittmeister—the order was clear enough—"

"Indeed it was a very triumph of clarity. It said to paint the planes—"

"It said to render them unobtrusive."

"—multicolored in order to obscure the character and shape, yes sir."

As Cargonico wound up to launch a tirade, another voice intervened, that of Von Hoeppner: "I think they've got you there, Cargonico. God knows they're multicolored. And whatever character or shape they may have is fairly well obscured."

"But this is—preposterous! Everyone in the Air Service knows that we are using brown and green lozenges for camouflaging our planes."

Richtofen stepped forward now. "I beg the major's pardon, but we are German soldiers—not female English Wrens. The Emperor may well command us to fight and perhaps die for the Fatherland, but no one has the right to command us to *hide*. Let the British hide!"

Cargonico looked helplessly at Von Hoeppner. Hoeppner stared back, unsympathetically. Cargonico shrugged, and the tension in the hangar was immediately broken. The newsmen rushed forward to question the pilots, and those who had photographic equipment began setting it up. Soon the inside of the hangar was illuminated by the noiseless explosions of the flash powder, and the planes were captured on plates, along with the pilots.

"Gentlemen," said the thoroughly beaten Major Carginico, "I approve your—your sentiments, of course. But this display, it's . . . fantastic. It's—"

"I'll tell you what it is," said the cynical Austrian newsman. "It's a veritable flying circus."

"That it is," said Cargonico, sighing ruefully. "That it is."

Chapter 8

A mud-slathered German infantryman, his battalion dug in a few hundred yards west of the aerodrome, stood in the trench holding a newspaper in his hand and gazing over the parapet at the planes taking off one-by-one. There was a photograph on the front page showing Richtofen and his grinning comrades in front of their newly painted planes. RICHTOFEN'S FLYING CIRCUS PLAYS IN ARENA OF DEATH WESTERN FRONT AWED BY ACES

"There goes Voss," said the infantryman. "And now Wolff ... There's the little Richtofen."

Other soldiers were watching too, and one of them took up the litany. "Hermann Goering ... and Udet ... And—"

"There he is! That's Richtofen himself!"

And they watched the blood-red Albatros D-V climb into the sky, envying him and the other pilots their clean, beautiful, noble style of war.

On the opposite side of No Man's Land, hundreds of British infantrymen were gazing upward as the Hawker Squadron droned overhead, and many of the soldiers had exactly the same thoughts of envy and admiration.

It was a clear and lovely morning, the sun just up, and Manfred von Richtofen felt fine. The ghoulish ghosts had been laid to rest and he was starting out anew, eager to confront the enemy he knew were aloft, as they were every clear morning like this. Passing over the sector of the Doumont salient, he glanced down at the stark moonscape below and caught a glimpse of the savage fighting down there. All he could actually see were a series of flashes—a concentrated artillery barrage—but he knew that men were being torn apart . . .

Richtofen raised his gloved hand and signaled the squadron to gain altitude, and the formation flared upward in perfect unison. Thus Richtofen banished the battlefield from his sight, and mind.

A minute later he spotted the Hawker Squadron far below, and almost at the same time Roy Brown spotted the German flight. Brown signaled to Hawker, and Hawker alerted the others.

And the classic dogfight began.

The Germans were already into their long power-dive, a single deadly thunderbolt, as the Hawker squadron rose to meet them. Richtofen, in the lead, veered to one side to catch a Spad on the left flank and send a spurt of bullets toward it. His aim was true, and the British plane began to break apart, one of its wings cracking and fluttering downward. Richtofen immediately lost interest in it, knowing it was doomed.

Roy Brown came up below a single-seater Halberstadt just as the German was firing a burst at a British plane. As it veered away, Brown caught it with a single long, devastating burst, the bullets smashing into the canvas-plywood bottom. Oil began to spew, soaking the shredded canvas, and the plane faltered. As Richtofen. had done, Brown instantly lost interest in the doomed plane.

Lanoe Hawker now spotted the target he had been looking for. Smiling to himself, he pulled his goggles down over his eyes and aimed his Spad and its Vickers guns at the target of his dreams.

Thus began one of the epic duels of the air, one that would be conjured up whenever combat veterans of the skies gathered to review the glorious past. There were literally hundreds of witnesses, and so the details of the battle are well known.

Richtofen saw a sudden line of tracers streaking past his plane on the right side. Turning his head sharply, he saw who it was that had him in his sights, and immediately he had skidded his Albatros into a wide loop that brought him to a position on Hawker's tail. Some of the soldiers below gasped at this almost unbelievable maneuver, and the speed with which it had been executed. For now the hunter had become the hunted, and Richtofen sent a stream of bullets into the Spad.

But the English ace of aces was not about to be trapped, for Hawker simply cut his engine and fell like a stone. As his flat plummeting started to become a dangerous, spinning fall, he gunned the engine and climbed out of trouble—with precisely the correct control and foreplanning to catch Richtofen once again in his sights.

The baron shook his head, impressed by the Englishman's skill. He had never witnessed a maneuver quite like that. But before Hawker could get off his next burst, Richtofen had jammed his rudder control with his boot and was out of reach.

Hermann Goering had been watching the duel through narrowed eyes, a twisted grin on his face. He found a certain perverse pleasure in realizing that at last Manfred von Richtofen had met his match. And in this moment of foolish reflection, Goering had opened himself to attack from the rear. A brand-new pilot named James Ridley had seen the German flying in a straight line, unaware, and had bored in for his first kill.

As the bullets came spurting into his left wing, Goering glanced furiously behind him and looped upward, falling off on his left wing—and coming in behind the inexperienced British pilot.

James Ridley realized to his dismay that he was outclassed. Fighting off panic, he tried to outmaneuver Goering; but it was impossible. Ridley began to turn cold in his own clammy sweat, for each time he made a maneuver, the relentless German pilot easily followed, and fired a short burst his way. They were short, teasing bursts, only two or three bullets at a time, and Ridley understood that the German was playing a terrible game with him. As each burst hit home, a portion of the plane broke away—either the wing wires, or the struts, or a piece of the wing itself.

Goering was enjoying himself hugely, moving his head from side to side as he fired each burst, as if keeping time to the music of death. The white-faced, sweating terror of his teenage victim only amused him.

At last a burst of fire smashed the Englishman's engine and the propeller slowed down to a stop, as gasoline and oil came spurting out into the airstream, atomizing it.

James Ridley had had enough. Looking back over his shoulder, he waved exaggeratedly to Goering, signaling surrender.

Unlike the others who had lost interest in a plane when it was obviously out of the fight, Goering continued to pursue the Englishman . . .

Hawker and Richtofen were still engaged in their immortal duel, neither man giving an inch, each man tortuously gaining the advantage long enough to get away a short burst before the other man escaped.

Lieutenant Brown caught sight of the duel as Richtofen once again came up behind Lanoe Hawker. Frowning, he flipped his plane over and headed toward his leader, intending to help out. But Hawker saw him coming up behind Richtofen, and waved him away angrily just as the Canadian was lining his plane up for a burst. Brown veered off at the last moment, seething with frustration.

James Ridley was bringing his smoking plane down for a crash landing along the edge of the Bois de Bailleul forest. It was going to be a close thing, for his plane was nearly out of control. Tensely the youngster dominated the sloppy controls until the plane was plowing up a long furrow of earth. In a veering skid at the end, with Ridley hanging on for dear life, the plane came to a flaming halt. Ridley climbed out groggily, dropped to the ground, and stumbled away as the flames licked the front half of the machine. There was a grin on his face, a grin of heartfelt gratitude for being alive—something he knew he wasn't necessarily entitled to after tangling with that superb German pilot up there in the unfriendly sky.

Ridley halted and turned to watch his plane burn. As he stood there, his ears picked up the sound of an aircraft engine growing louder with alarming speed. Puzzled, he glanced upward.

And when he caught sight of Goering's Halberstadt it was already too late.

In his long dive, Goering could clearly see the young man in the open—small, petrified, and helpless. Goering's right hand, gauntleted in black leather, moved off the control column and up to the trigger of the Spandau machine gun. A second later bullets were raising dust all around Ridley, and four of them had passed cleanly through his body.

When Goering's plane winked out of sight over the treetops, Ridley lay dead on the ground, his eyes wide-open, his arms outspread in the dirt as if he were pleading with someone.

Ernst Udet had seen it all and watched Goering climb away from the site of his abominable deed. When Goering saw him watching, he banked close to Udet until they were flying on a parallel course. Goering glared steadily at his friend, his face filled with threat.

The magnificent duel was still under way, as hundreds of soldiers watched far below. The situation now was positively electrifying, for Hawker and Richtofen were locked in a continuous loop no more than three hundred yards in diameter, and it would have been deadly for either adversary to break the circle. The two men were directly opposite one another, and could easily see each other's face.

Hawker, always the debonair gentleman, casually waved at the German. The baron broke into a surprised smile, and raised his gloved hand in an answering salute.

And for one second Lanoe Hawker had let his guard down. Richtofen knew instinctively that his worthy adversary's fighting spirit had been momentarily neutralized by the friendly little exchange—so human, so charming. But while he was in the air, Richtofen was virtually inhuman. And Richtofen possessed the killer instinct that Hawker did not.

In the twinkling of an eye, Richtofen had jerked his Albatros out of the locked circle, was cutting across the chord of the circle, and was lining up the unready Englishman in the sights of his twin Spandaus. The crosshairs crept past the tail and down the fuselage until they merged with the back of Lanoe Hawker's head, and Richtofen squeezed the trigger. Tracers lanced out, their parallel lines closing slowly on the Englishman's head.

Slowly.

Or so it seemed to the baron, and so he would recall it afterwards in his waking hours and in his nightmares. First the bullets blasted the fuselage behind Hawker's head and then, ever so slowly, they struck the head itself and a gummy slow spray of blood and bone flared out into the slipstream and was sucked backward into vanishment. Slowly the helmet disintegrated, and slowly the goggles, until there was nothing left, and it seemed to Richtofen that the man's entire body was starting to ooze in bloody red syrup all down the rear of the fuselage.

Finally he took his hand off the trigger and wrenched his eyes off the incredible horror before him. The Spad slowly turned over and began to dive downward.

A sudden burst of tracers from behind him snapped Richtofen out of his stunned freeze, and he flicked the controls into a dive. It was Lieutenant Gerald Murphy, his helmet off, his eyes blazing like a madman's, bent on revenge. He nearly rammed Richtofen in his insane fury; the baron barely managed to avoid him.

And then the whole show was over. By an unseen impulse, an undirected order from some mysterious force, both units backed away from each other, regrouped, and flew in formation back to their respective bases.

And when the Richtofen squadron landed a few minutes later, the same German soldiers in the same trenches watched them with awe and envy, and even a little jealousy. Such a neat, clean way to fight a war!

Roy Brown stood heartbroken for a moment beside his plane, helmet and goggles in his hand. Then he turned and walked across the field toward his quarters, his shoulders slumped in dejection. No one saw him for the rest of the day—until supper.

There were a number of empty chairs that night in the officers' mess. The most conspicuous was the one at the head of the long table, the place where Lanoe Hawker had eaten so many meals and drunk so many toasts and enjoyed so many hours of good fellowship

with his friends. But now it was empty and the silent
pilots ate their food half-heartedly and avoided looking
at one end of the table. Nobody felt much like eating
anyway, even though everyone was making the effort to
keep up appearances. And nobody felt like talking.

Brown's place was empty too, but the glass of stale
wine was still sitting there.

Now the door opened and in came Irish Gerald
Murphy, followed by a grim-visaged Wing Commander
Owen. Murphy took his seat and began to eat, casting
furtive glances at the empty place at the head of the
table. The Wing Commander stood behind Hawker's
chair for a moment, his hand on it and the men could
see he was having difficulty controlling himself. He
opened his mouth to speak, but then swallowed and
looked down at the floor.

Forks were put down softly, as the men stared down
at their plates. It was Gerald Murphy who finally
broke the spell of grief.

"He didn't even have to fly, you know. The old man
wanted him out of it—isn't that true, sir?" Owen
nodded in misery. "Whoever heard of a major flying.
He could be sitting here now."

The door opened and Brown walked in. He had been
drinking. His ulcer was obviously bothering him
mightily, for he approached the table bent over like an
old man. The pilots watched him as he slowly made his
way to his chair, his lips clamped shut over the stab-
bing pains in his stomach.

Roy Brown reached down and picked up the glass of
stale wine and raised it to his lips and drank it slowly.

Then, with infinite ceremony and a look of grief on his face, he bowed to the empty chair at the head of the table. Putting the empty glass back on the table, upside down, he departed, bent over like an old man.

Chapter 9

"Rittmeister Baron von Richtofen, stand before His Majesty, the Emperor!"

Richtofen stepped forward, marching stiffly in place until he was two paces in front of the Kaiser himself. In the background, the Brandenburg Gate loomed imposingly, the breeze whipping a stand of flags on top. Down below, the entire Richtofen squadron was drawn up in formation. A crowd of civilians pushed against the barricades to witness the ceremony.

Kaiser Wilhelm stepped forward, plucked a beribboned medal from the outstretched hand of an aide, and carefully placed it around the young airman's neck. He grasped Richtofen's hand and shook it vigorously.

"It's fine, killing the English up there, isn't it?"

Richtofen was stunned by the bloodthirsty question, and he stared down at the thin, popeyed man.

"As you say, Your Majesty."

"I only wish I could be with you. The hardest part of the war, for me, is not being up at the front with my stout fellows."

It shocked Richtofen to realize that the man who controlled Germany's destiny, the man who was his own royal and supreme leader was—dare he say it? a fool! An undignified fool!

"Of course, Your Majesty."

"They betrayed us, you know. The British sold us like cabbages to the French. They're not fit for empire—but we'll see to that, won't we?" And he leered broadly into Richtofen's face.

"Whatever you say, Your Majesty."

"Go back now, Richtofen. Go back and butcher another forty of those dogs. Do you hear?"

"Whatever you say, Your Majesty."

They shook hands once more and that was the end of the conversation.

Richtofen did his best to put it out of his mind. He had a duty to perform, a simple straight-forward duty. That was all he had to worry about. Nothing else mattered.

But he found that he could not dismiss it so easily—this shocking discovery that the Kaiser was a silly little fool.

Later in the day, Richtofen lay stretched out on the bed in his hotel room, smoking a cigaret and trying to sort it all out. Beside him lay a newspaper with the headline: ACE OF ACES HONORED BY KAISER. Did it really matter in the least that the Emperor talked like a bloodthirsty fool to him that morning? He decided—without thinking too hard about it—that it did not matter at all. In his warrior's heart Richtofen believed his duty was to shoot Englishmen out of the sky. Maybe the Emperor was right, after all! He *would* go back to the war and shoot down another forty of the sons of bitches.

He felt a lot better.

Hearing a noise out in the street, he swung his legs off the bed and stood up. Looking out the window he saw a crowd below, and they saw him. A cheer went up. Richtofen smiled, pleased at the greeting, and waved once before stepping backward out of sight. One could not stand there all day waving, like the Pope!

He lifted his new and very precious medal off the table and held it up to look at it. The *Pour le Merité* was not awarded casually, he knew—only to the bravest of the brave. Feeling suddenly immodest, he put the medal back down.

There was a light knock on the door. Richtofen, glad of the interruption, walked over and opened it. There stood a small, gray-haired man with thick glasses, holding his hat in one hand and a small case in the other.

"Herr Baron . . . that is, Rittmeister."

"Either will do," said Richtofen politely.

"The guard said it would be all right," said the man.

"Come in, come in. Perhaps you'd like to explain it to me as well as the guard."

"I'm Funck, sir—from Berlin? I've brought your—"

"Of course! You're the jeweler."

Funck put the case down on the table and opened it. He took out five of the small sterling silver cups Richtofen had been receiving regularly by mail to commemorate his victories. "I—you will pardon me if I say . . ."

"Yes?"

"I only want to say what a privilege it is to supply

you with these trophies, sir. I feel, when I read of your exploits, that somehow I am there, in the sky with you . . ."

Richtofen looked at the little man and was touched by his earnest sincerity. "That's good of you to say. Thank you very much."

The jeweler bowed and departed. Richtofen closed the door, smiling, and walked back to the table where the five cups stood—each representing a victory.

His smile suddenly died.

For each represented also a horrible death.

But he must forget that. He must!

That night Manfred von Richtofen attended a gala affair that turned out to be perhaps the greatest evening of his short life.

He had been invited to a ball at the Fokker mansion. Anthony Fokker was known throughout Europe as an authentic technological genius; he had invented some of the German Air Force's finest planes. Tonight he was to play the role of super-salesman, but his guest of honor would not learn of this until late in the evening.

When Richtofen arrived, fashionably late, the ball was in full swing. The tuxedoed band was playing a Viennese waltz and the dancing couples all seemed young and beautiful and dynamically alive. One would hardly know there was a war on. The baron paused for a moment at the entrance to the grand ballroom and took in the impressive scene. His eye fell on three huge photographs at the far end of the room. Kaiser Wilhelm II in the middle, with Oswald Boelcke and Manfred von Richtofen on either side. The pictures were draped in the national colors, with the Hohenzollern eagle above. Smiling now, Richtofen watched his younger brother charming several giggling young ladies. And there was Wolff—being bored by a big, overbearing matron in brocade. And over there, the stocky Goering, leering lustfully at a comely young maiden standing beside an alabaster statue of Venus. Just before stepping into the great room, he saw Udet and Voss talking in one corner—and there was something incongruous about them. Richtofen stared for a couple of seconds before he realized that they were engaged in an intense, almost angry discussion. Their intensity was distinctly out of place in the gay atmosphere that swirled around them. Udet was telling Voss something, and Voss was shaking his head in disbelief and disgust.

Then the music stopped and the band began to play *Deutschland Uber Alles* as the guest of honor was recognized.

Colonel von Hoeppner stepped forward to meet the young hero, with the host close behind.

"It's marvelous, Richtofen! In a few hours you've captured Berlin."

"Only a temporary occupation, Major . . . I beg your pardon, *Colonel*. Tomorrow the capital will belong to the bureaucrats again."

Hoeppner smiled and turned to the man beside him. "Let me present your host, Anthony Fokker. Next to you, he's the most important man in the Air Service."

Fokker, in formal evening clothes, festooned with various Orders of the Empire, smoothly welcomed the guest. "Welcome to my home, Herr Rittmeister. You've been a long time coming."

"I beg your pardon?"

Fokker waved his white-gloved hand expansively about the decorated ballroom. "They've all been here—Immelmann, Boelcke, Schroeder. We spent many hours talking about war planes and the problems of flying them, as well as building them . . ."

"Your planes are famous, Herr Fokker, and well they deserve to be."

". . . but I've always wanted to talk to *you*. To sound you out and draw on your experience, and perhaps show you some new ideas."

"I'd enjoy that. I'm sure there must be better planes than the ones we've been flying."

Anthony Fokker's handsome, aging playboy face took on a crafty look, and he said: "Perhaps I can show you one."

"*Show* me one, Herr Fokker?"

"Later in the evening, perhaps. In the meantime, allow me to be mysterious about it."

And they both laughed as the host led his guest of honor toward the champagne table.

Voss and Wolff and some of the other pilots were sitting at a table with a number of extraordinarily good-looking women, and when Baron von Richtofen approached they raised a raucous greeting and somewhat rudely made a place for him among the admiring females. The baron sat down, holding his glass of champagne.

But before he could relax and drink in the lovely sights all around him, Werner Voss leaned over to whisper loudly in his ear.

"We've got trouble."

Richtofen stiffened. "News from France?"

Voss grinned sardonically. "You could call it that, I suppose. A delayed dispatch—regarding our portly comrade, Lieutenant Hermann Goering."

Richtofen looked at Voss. "Well? What is it?"

And Voss told his leader what Ernst Udet had seen at the edge of the Bois de Bailleul forest a few days earlier, keeping his voice low so the others could not hear.

Richtofen was angrier than he had been before in his life. As leader of the squadron, he felt his very soul had been befouled by Goering's incredible act of deliberately killing a grounded enemy pilot. The honor of the squadron had been compromised, and there was no way of removing the stain.

As Richtofen sat staring across the dance floor at the unsuspecting Goering, the lights suddenly went out and everything went black.

A small spotlight snapped on. Caught in its soft white glare, at the edge of the bandstand, stood a beautiful blonde in a blood-red dress. Accompanied softly by the orchestra, she began to sing.

The warriors of the sky, our men of destiny ...

She stepped down and began to move sinuously among the tables. Her low and smoky voice had an obvious effect on everyone present. The song, for all its glorification of war, had a poignant air about it and sobered the guests.

The young men of sorrow and glory, their sacrifice worthy of eternal Valhalla ...

Manfred von Richtofen had forgotten about Goering, and indeed everything else, and was listening and watching the woman, entranced, as she slowly made her way toward him. It was obvious to everyone that she was singing her haunting ballad for the guest of honor himself.

Your Fatherland's gratitude is eternal as well, But the earthbound mortals will never understand The ecstasy of war in the air . . .

When the strange song had ended, the lights came on, and the young blonde stood motionless as the alabaster statue of Venus, directly in front of Richtofen.

As in a trance, he rose and took her in his arms and they began to dance to the soft strains of a more familiar ballad, searching each other's eyes, oblivious to the glittering world about them.

The garden was the formal kind, with Greek and Roman deities, shepherds and shepherdesses in the *sans souci* manner of Frederick the Great. Richtofen and the woman strolled leisurely through it, carrying their champagne glasses with them. The blonde singer stopped to touch a white flower. Richtofen plucked it off for her, removed one of his ribbons from his chest, and used its pin to attach the flower to her blood-red dress.

"I don't even know your name," he said softly.

"It is Ilse." She suddenly whirled from him, coy and beguiling. "If you could be anywhere right now," she asked, "where would you choose?"

"Why, right here," said Richtofen, surprised. "Where else?"

"That's a pretty compliment. You wouldn't rather be in London or Paris as a conquerer?"

He shook his head. "I leave that to the professional conquerers."

She looked at him, a glint in her eye. "Don't you know that everyone dreams that you'll take all Germany to London and to Paris and to—"

Richtofen broke out laughing. "You make me sound like a cross between the Orient Express and a channel steamer!"

Anthony Fokker suddenly appeared on the other side of the garden, walking quickly toward them.

"Well, I see you've gotten acquainted," he said. "Excellent! By the way, Richtofen, I wonder if you'd be so good as to make a small trip with me?"

Involuntarily the young baron cast a glance toward Ilse, and Fokker hastened to reassure him: "The fraulein is invited as well, needless to say."

Without waiting for their answer he turned and walked through a gate in the hedge and proceeded along the graveled pathway leading to the front of the mansion. His chauffeur waited there beside the Mercedes. Richtofen and Ilse followed in silence, wondering what was in store for them.

Arbenz-dohl Aerodrome was dark except for an isolated guardhouse beside the gate. The uniformed guard saluted Fokker smartly as the three visitors walked through. A hundred yards inside the field, a dark hangar loomed before them in the night, and a helmeted guard stepped in front of them with his rifle at the ready.

"Good," said Fokker. "You're wide awake."

The guard lowered the weapon and stepped inside the hangar and, without instructions, snapped on a light switch.

"And here," said Fokker, gesturing expansively with one outstretched arm, "is a new Pegasus that could carry you to greater glory."

Directly before them, illuminated by one brilliant spotlight, perched the new DR-1 Fokker Triplane, almost perfect in its lethal beauty. It was painted silver and gleamed coolly under the light. It was without insignia, an anonymous object of mechanical art.

"My God," said Richtofen in a choked voice, "it's—"

"Go on, say it. It's not a sin for a soldier to recognize it. It's beautiful."

"Yes."

"I didn't plan it to be beautiful, you know. I planned it for speed, and for stability. To supply the best pilots of the Empire with a machine they could depend on. But somehow—I still don't understand how—it came out beautiful."

"Yes," said Richtofen, and the blonde Ilse heard a note of passion in his voice. It irritated her. This masculine admiration for a mere machine, she felt, would be better directed at another kind of beauty.

"You work on something for so long," Fokker was saying, "that you stop seeing it, in a sense. You just keep working, and then one day—"

Ilse couldn't stand this any longer. She strode forward into the light, her red dress swinging gently around her long legs, and it was hard for the two men to keep their attention on the Triplane.

"—and then one day you see it's far more than you had in mind at the start. You see that it's—it's . . ."

"Lovely," said the baron.

Ilse heard him utter the word, but couldn't be sure if he was talking about the stupid machine—or her. Now she posed deliberately, almost blatantly, against the tapering silver fuselage, holding her pose for a moment before moving gracefully into a different pose altogether.

"How long to build her?" asked Richtofen.

"Not as long as you'd think. A few failures, a near miss or two, that's all."

The blonde Ilse stood still, hands on hips, glaring at the DR-1 as if it were a despised rival.

"Is she fast?" asked the baron.

"Fast enough, but it's the maneuverability that makes her special."

Ilse was standing beside the tail assembly, running her hand over the stabilizer surface as if looking for dust. She turned and gazed toward the two men, her eyes opaque and unreadable.

"I had trouble with that tail," said Fokker.

Ilse now moved forward until she came up against the lower of the three wings. Leaning forward, she rested her arms on the top surface of the middle wing and froze in an artificial but wholly charming pose.

"Will she stall?" asked the Baron.

"Of course—if you want her to. She'll fall into a spin and out again at a touch."

Richtofen and Anthony Fokker exploded with simultaneous laughter that echoed around the hangar and startled Ilse, as they were finally overcome by the crescendo of *double entendre* implicit in their remarks. Ilse smirked to herself, hugely flattered.

Richtofen became serious again. "How about the response, Herr Fokker?"

"The response? Fabulous. I've tried it, you know. She's up to anything you could require."

The woman stepped up onto a small platform and looked into the cockpit, and reached down to touch the control stick. As she fondled it, her face took on the dreamy expression of one engaged in love-play.

"If you intended to pique my interest, Herr Fokker— you've succeeded."

"I had hoped so, Herr Rittmeister. I wanted you to be the first pilot to try her."

And now Ilse was staring at the young airman, aiming his way a torrid look of the most intense yearning.

"You know," said Richtofen, with a straight face, "she looks quite dangerous."

"Not to *you,* my friend. She—if I may say it—she's your meat. You can handle her, I assure you."

And now Ilse was walking slowly toward Richtofen, and her desire for him moved ahead of her like a wave of heat. When finally the two of them were facing each other, gazing into one another's faces, Fokker coughed politely and said: "Well. So. I'll leave you two here to look over my lady."

Whether he meant the plane or the woman he didn't say. When Richtofen looked around, he was gone. His receding footsteps sounded from the tarmac outside.

Richtofen took the blonde singer gently by the arm and led her toward the cubicle-office in one corner of the hangar.

"He jabbers a great deal, doesn't he?" the woman asked.

"Well, after all, he was trying to sell me—"

"Did you need to be sold?"

Richtofen looked slightly embarrassed. "It's—a very lovely piece of design."

"Thank you," she said, smirking devilishly at him.

There was a bottle of Napoleon brandy and two tapered glasses on the desk inside. Richtofen looked surprised. Ilse did not.

"Fokker's manager has remarkable taste," said the baron.

"And a pocketbook to match," the blonde singer added.

Richtofen poured a little brandy into the glasses, gave one to Ilse, and picked up the other.

"To beauty . . ."

Ilse smiled, and they each took a sip. She put down her glass and reached toward him softly and began to unbutton his tunic, button by button. It was more than he could stand, for she unbuttoned him slowly. He pushed her hands aside and finished it himself, as she began to shed her blood-red dress.

"We *could* go back," she said tauntingly. "Herr Fokker must have a private room somewhere in his mansion."

"This is private enough," said Richtofen.

They moved into each other's arms and clung nakedly for a moment before moving at last toward the couch.

And behind them, poised in the middle of the hangar floor, the DR-1 Triplane gleamed silver in the spotlight.

Chapter 10

Lieutenant Roy Brown was sipping a glass of mineral water in a pathetic little bistro at the edge of the ruined village near the aerodrome. Behind him, two British soldiers were having a game of darts, pausing now and then for a pull on their pints. An old Frenchman, his evil-smelling dog asleep at his feet, sat staring into space at one of the tables.

The silence was shattered when the door burst open and in came several more pilots from the aerodrome. Brown turned his head and saw Irish Gerald Murphy and Fred Thompson among them. When Murphy and Thompson saw the young Canadian at the bar, they turned away coldly.

The last man to enter was a slender, dark-haired fellow in a Royal Canadian Air Force uniform. He too looked at Roy Brown, who had turned back to the bar, but the newcomer didn't turn away like the others.

"Brown?" He took a step closer. "Is that Roy Brown?"

He reached out and put his hand on Brown's shoulder, and Brown whirled angrily on him. But then the sour face turned to one of wonder and then delight.

"Wop May! What the hell are you doing here?"

May threw back his head and laughed. "You didn't really expect me to leave the whole war to *you*, did you?"

"But I thought—"

"—I was in school? I was—until one of my teachers said this would be the last war, and that after this one ended, 'war' would be nothing but a word in the textbooks."

Brown didn't know quite what to say. So he said nothing.

"What're you drinking, Roy? I'll buy you another."

"This is mineral water, but—"

"Mineral water?"

"—I just wanted a sip or two. I'm having a spot of trouble with my stomach. Listen, I was just about to leave. Why don't you stroll with me a way."

When they were out on the road, Wop May began to elaborate on why he had quit school to join up. ". . . so you see, Roy, I *had* to come. I mean, we'll be the last soldiers, won't we? The other generations are going to envy us, you see. They—"

"Wop, this isn't a game. Believe me."

"But Roy, I mean, look at it this way—"

Brown stopped and touched the youngster's sleeve. His face was dead serious. "Wop, if you want to think it's a game, all right. But it's the kind where when they catch you off base—they kill you."

May looked at him doubtfully. "Come on, now. There are rules, after all. We've left the Dark Ages behind us."

They were approaching the end of the airfield now,

and Roy Brown gazed out across the flight line where several Spads and Camels and De Havilands were lined up. "There are no rules, I tell you. Not any more. That's all past."

"What are you saying, Roy?"

"A week ago, the sons of bitches machine gunned a man on the ground, completely defenseless—a pilot from our squadron."

May's jaw dropped in astonishment. "I never heard of anything like that."

"You will from now on. That's the way things are."

There was a two-seater De Haviland coming in for a landing, and they paused to watch. Brown suddenly saw that the plane's undercarriage was damaged. Barely hanging from the underside of the plane, it swung from side to side. They watched in stunned horror as the plane touched down, plowed along for a short way, took a horrendous flip and went crashing straight into the flight line. The whole mass of wreckage came to a halt only twenty-five yards from where the two men stood rooted.

Brown was the first to reach the wreck. He plunged in, determined to extricate the pilot. Crewmen appeared on the run to give him a hand, but by the time they arrived, he knew the pilot was beyond help. Wop May was trying furiously to pull the observer out of the mangled front seat.

"You're wasting your time. Wop."

"I've almost got him!"

"He's dead."

"But you haven't even—"

"I don't need to. Look at his eyes, Wop."

A few minutes later they watched as the two bodies were loaded aboard the ambulance.

"Their names were Kenyon and Siebert," said Roy Brown, glaring at the young man beside him. "Do you reckon they'll make your textbooks, Wop?"

But May was far too shaken to answer. The two of them turned away and started walking across the field. Passing the tall silent figure of Wing Commander Owen, they both snapped a regulation salute his way. Owen fell into step beside them, his hands clasped behind his back, his head down.

"He was a good man, Kenyon," said the Wing Commander. "His brother died with Kitchener. Siebert was one of our best."

Brown noticed how tired, how old, how drained of spirit the wing commander seemed.

"How many men can we lose, and . . . keep going?"

"Maybe we'll find out, Wing Commander. When we run out of Kenyons and Sieberts."

Owen nodded and studied Brown narrowly for a moment. "Mr. Brown, I've been meaning to speak to you about a certain matter."

"Sir?"

"Some of the other pilots seem to feel that your— your *gesture* with the wine the other evening was disrespectful to Major Hawker."

Brown felt a hot flush of anger come into his face, but he kept his lips clamped until calm returned. "They're wrong, but it doesn't matter. If they want to toast Richtofen and his miserable gang again, I'll be glad to stay clear of the mess."

Wing Commander Owen smiled without humor. "I

doubt if they'll be toasting the Germans again. That's one point you succeeded in making."

"Well, it's not the point I set out to make."

"Brown, one day the world will look back, and—"

The Canadian interrupted him sharply. "Commander, the world has *changed*. The knights have all been deflowered."

Owen winced a little, but answered: "We're still soldiers."

"Which is to say, killers."

Owen shook his head, visibly shaken. "I—I loved Lanoe Hawker. We believed in the same things. We belonged to that other world, the world of order and restraint and honor and decency."

Wop May, listening intently, nodded sympathetically at the wing commander's words.

"And now, without him," Owen went on, "there's no one to see us through."

Softly, savagely, Roy Brown spoke. "Commander, there never was a Hawker."

Owen's reaction was a confused frown.

"He was a good man," Brown said, "and only that. You dreamed up a myth and expected him to carry us all through Hell itself on his own strength. But things aren't done that way any more. I'm not sure they ever were."

Stubbornly Owen persisted: "We need more men like—"

"Damn it, *we need each other,*" Brown said passionately. "We need to stop looking for someone to lead us. The kings and the princes and the heroes are falling. Europe is done with them. There are only men left, just plain human beings. Just Kenyons and Sieberts and Murphys and Browns and Mays. If we can't win with them, Commander, there's no other way."

They walked in silence for a while, moving slowly across the grass, and Roy Brown wondered if he had gone too far. It was twilight now, and the shadow of the operations hut reached halfway across the airfield toward them. Finally Owen spoke.

"I suspect that's why I despise you a little, Brown."

Brown looked over at the older man, aghast. "Sir?"

"Because you make it impossible for me to see any other way, either. And I don't *want* to see it your way. If my way is an illusion, then so be it."

With a curt nod to each man, he turned and walked off toward his quarters.

"This is an official interview, Lieutenant. You will stand at strict attention. You will answer the questions put to you, and you will make no statement until one is required of you."

Hermann Goering pulled himself to attention, his hands at his sides, his chin tucked in, his eyes boring straight into the wall behind his interrogator's head. Manfred von Richtofen, seated at the desk, regarded him with contempt. In the corner of the room sat an enlisted man, taking everything down in shorthand.

"Let us begin. I am informed that during a recent flight near the village of Le Hamel, on the edge of the Bois de Bailleul, you shot down an English S.E.5a scout craft. Is that correct?"

Goering's pudgy face tightened, his mouth working.

He knew he was on dangerous ground. "Yes, sir, I did. I did shoot down such a plane."

"And did the pilot survive the crash?"

Richtofen could see that the lieutenant was beginning to sweat, as a single drop rolled down one side of his face.

"Yes," said Goering. "Yes, I—if I'm not mistaken . . ."

Richtofen rose from his chair and walked around the end of the desk until he was standing next to the stiff, quivering man. Goering continued to stare straight ahead.

"Lieutenant Goering, this indirection is unseemly in a German officer. I want you to answer *yes* or *no* to my questions. Is that clear?"

"Yes, sir!"

Richtofen stepped closer until he was practically speaking in Goering's ear. "Let us continue, then. Did you, when you saw the English pilot was still alive and had escaped from his burning plane, did you then make a pass at him and strafe him to death as he stood helpless on the ground?"

Goering's sensuous mouth was working furiously now, and his cheeks were shining with sweat.

"Well?" demanded Richtofen. "It's a perfectly simple question. A German officer should be able to answer it even before it is asked. *Did you fire on a crashed pilot?*"

"Sir . . . the man, he fired at me."

"What's that?"

"He was armed with a pistol, and . . . as I flew past, he—"

"What were you doing there in the first place?"

"I wanted to confirm my victory, sir—that's all."

"Go on."

"Well, as I said—he fired three shots at me."

Richtofen glared at him, his lip curled in contempt. "So it was self-defense, is that it?"

Goering nodded vigorously, his eyes very wide.

"I commend you, Goering, on your escape from such a formidable foe. And by the way: What evidence can you produce to back this claim?"

"Evidence, sir? Why, you have my word."

The angry baron spoke directly into Goering's ear, his voice soft and menacing. "Yes, I have your word. I have that, and the British have a pilot shot to pieces after he was *hors de combat*. And I would trade with them in a minute."

"Sir—"

"Listen to me. If I hear of such a thing again—even a rumor—I'll break you. I'll put every bit of prestige I have on the line. I'll call in favors. I'll go to the Emperor himself to see you shot. Do you hear me, Goering?"

"Yes, sir."

"This squadron is made up of gentlemen. We fight as gentlemen. We hunt as gentlemen. We are not butchers. *We are not butchers!*"

Richtofen was nearly beside himslf with anger. Lieutenant Goering's knees were beginning to tremble. The baron whirled and took two steps away, and then once more faced the sweating, trembling man.

"You are dismissed."

Hermann Goering, his eyes wide, almost ran out of

the room. The enlisted man folded up his pad and quietly left, closing the door behind him. Richtofen went over to the window and gazed at the sky.

I wonder how many of the others would do what Goering did, he asked himself.

The noise of the Vickers machine guns was positively deafening. Roy Brown sat behind one, firing short bursts into a large white target three hundred yards across the firing range. Wop May stood behind him, arms crossed, watching closely. A few yards down the firing line, Gerald Murphy was having trouble with his gun. It kept misfiring. He would pull the trigger and get off a burst of two rounds and that was it. Angrily he yanked the bolt back and forth, clearing the weapon, and pulled the trigger again—and again, after a burst of two rounds, the gun went dead. The other pilots stood behind Murphy, glancing occasionally over at Roy Brown, intrigued at the way he had his Vickers working.

Brown sat back, released his hold on the weapon, and wiped his face with a handkerchief.

"Roy, it's amazing," said May, stepping forward. "No jamming at all."

Brown nodded and stuffed the handkerchief back into his pocket. "We can save the practice cartridges and hand-load them with powder in our spare time. If the powder load is constant, there'll be very few stoppages, believe me." He moved aside and motioned May behind the gun. "Give it a try, why don't you."

Wop May sat down, put both feet on either side of the gun-mount, grasped the hand-holds, aimed at the distant target, and squeezed off a long burst. The tracers zoomed gracefully into the target.

The other Vickers was silent. Murphy had been watching Brown and May with envy. Now he climbed to his feet, dusted off the seat of his pants, and walked over toward them. The other pilots followed. May held up his firing.

"A regular powder monkey, aren't you, Brown? A regular master of ordnance."

Brown looked at him coldly. "I've been loading my own shells and belts for weeks, and I'm alive. So I suppose in a way that does make me a master of ordnance."

Fred Thompson scratched his chin dubiously and said: "Major Hawker left that sort of thing to the mechanics."

Quickly Brown snatched an empty brass cartridge out of the dust and held it up. "There's your Major Hawker. A spent shell."

Gerald Murphy's face was darkened with outrage. He took a step forward and cocked his right arm to take a swing at Brown—but May reached out and held that arm in an iron grip.

Brown casually picked up the belt of live ammunition, one end already feeding into the Vickers' receiver, and held it up. "This is the squadron. If it's properly used, it can go a long way toward helping end this war."

Murphy relaxed, and May let go of his arm. Murphy was listening with a quizzical look on his face. "What the hell are you getting at?"

"Just this. We're all linked together. We live and we

die together. Is one bullet better than another?" He glanced at the pilots and shook his head. "Of course not. As long as it fires, it's the same as the rest."

Brown brandished the end of the belt of live ammo in Gerald Murphy's face. "Which one is the hero, Murphy? Can you tell me that? Which one is marked for Richtofen?"

Fred Thompson stared sourly at Brown. "We're not shells, Brown. We're men, and—"

"Yes, and that's what gets us killed. Our guns and our planes fail sometimes—but mostly it's we who fail. In a way, we are machines too—and if we fail to be efficient machines, we die."

The men were looking at Brown in a new way now, listening hard, wanting to understand. But Gerald Murphy was fighting it, and his Irish face reflected the inner struggle.

"Damn you, Brown," he said. "Damn you."

"He's right, Murphy," said Wop May quietly.

The other pilots nodded. Murphy looked at them and shook his head in confusion. Pushing May aside, he suddenly plopped down behind the Vickers, jacked a shell into the chamber, and squeezed off a burst, and another, and another, his face twisted in frustration and confusion and rage. The rest of the men stood there and watched him blast the distant target to shreds until the ammunition belt ran through the hot receiver and the gun fell silent.

Murphy slumped over the gunsight as if he was exhausted. Then, in a croaking voice, he spoke.

"You want us to forget that we're human. All right, damn you—I've forgotten."

"That isn't the point," Brown protested. "I only want you to see what you're here for. To *kill*. And you can't devote yourself to killing and be a gentleman at the same time."

Murphy slowly raised his head and looked at Brown. "Go on."

Intense now, filled with an urge to get his blunt message across to the pilots, Roy Brown turned to face them. "When the job is killing, you must imitate the best killers."

"For example?" asked Thompson.

"Wolves, Mr. Thompson. Wolves!"

Thompson looked puzzled. "I understand they—"

"They hunt in packs," said Gerald Murphy, gazing at the young Canadian with something close to real respect.

Chapter 11

It had been a long time since Werner Voss sat in the baron's strange room. It was different. There was a wolf's head mounted on the wall above the bunk, and the rest of the wall space was almost entirely covered with Richtofen's souvenirs—fragments of planes, machine guns, and even a pilot's leather helmet. There was a bizarre chandelier suspended from the ceiling now, made from the rotary engine of a wrecked Sopwith Camel, fitted with lights. The sterling silver cups were everywhere—the mantel, tables, chairs.

There were fifty-five of them.

Voss, dressed in his flying suit, sat on the dilapidated sofa with a cigaret in one hand and a glass of wine in the other. He did not look at all like a man who had just announced his imminent death.

Richtofen was standing in the middle of the room, pulling on his flying suit, his face a tight mask of pain. "Are you certain, Werner?"

"The diagnosis is final. Six months, possibly. No more than a year at the outside."

"That's ridiculous," said Richtofen with sudden heat.

"He's a quack. Nothing is final. We can have you in Berlin in five hours. They—"

"Stop it, Richtofen. He's the man who taught them in Berlin. He knows terminal tuberculosis as if he'd invented it."

Richtofen jammed his fist into his palm. "There's *got* to be—"

Voss held up his hand, the one with the cigaret, and silently asked Richtofen to stop. He seemed utterly unmoved by his impending death. "I don't want to die in a hospital. Have you ever seen anyone die in a hospital? Nowadays they put tubes . . ." He paused and made a face. "Ach, it's disgusting." He looked up at Richtofen, a long hard look, filled with meaning. "I want to keep flying, Richtofen. You can see that."

"Of course you'll fly. You'll fly as long as—" And he stopped. "Werner! You don't mean to—"

"Kill myself? Don't be a fool. But I will no longer be afraid of death in the air."

"You will be reckless?"

"Perhaps. But I will kill like fury itself, for I myself am as good as dead."

"I don't understand you."

"Don't try. There's no logic to it. I shall kill because I am dying—and if I could, I'd kill the whole world. It drives me crazy to know that when I am ashes, some man will look into some woman's eyes." Werner Voss was no longer cool and calm; his face was transfigured by the passion of his utterance. "Can you understand?"

Richtofen shook his head helplessly. "I don't want to understand."

Voss laughed bitterly.

"I am the new kind of soldier. Because I'm as good as dead, there's nothing to lose. It will give me profound pleasure to kill. There was no pleasure to it before—it was merely a duty."

Abruptly Voss put down his glass, snubbed out his cigaret and rose.

"I'm deeply sorry, my friend," said Richtofen.

"Forget it!" He walked to the door and turned. "I'm ashamed of what I've become. That changes nothing, but I do regret it. The old days are gone." He shook his head and smiled to himself, and departed.

Richtofen finished buttoning his flying suit. Under his breath he muttered aloud, "The old days are *not* gone. Maybe gone for you, Werner, but not the rest of my men."

He flung open the door and stalked out into the dawn.

Although neither group knew it, the German pilots and the British pilots were both listening to last-minute instructions at the same time, separated as they were by twenty-seven miles of muddy barren battlefield.

Manfred von Richtofen stood before his Fokker Triplane outlined against the dawning sky. His face was hard.

"No matter what you've heard, no matter what your opinion of the matter, I expect every one of you to fight as Boelcke would have had us fight." He looked into their faces one by one, beginning to stand out in the morning light. "Does anyone question this?"

The men shuffled restively. No one dared even think of rebelling, but none were pleased by their leader's insistance on the standards of the old code. Finally, one of the newer pilots spoke up.

"Sir, there are rumors that the British executed a captured flyer from one of the other squadrons."

"There are rumors that the dead will rise on the last day, too. I will wait and see. In the meantime, you will do your duty—neither less, nor more. Pilots, man your planes!"

Twenty-seven miles away, Roy Brown was speaking. "Stay very close on the leader. We'll fly *en masse,* and stay that way. When the fight commences, hold your fire until you get your sights lined up on the *man.* They have plenty of planes, but pilots are another matter."

Now Murphy spoke up. "You still want us to stake out the old De Havillands as bait?"

"It's a risk, I know, but it will bring the Germans sniffing around. And with any luck, we'll blast the sons of bitches out of the sky. Let's go!"

Richtofen was enjoying the brilliant dawn. He sat strapped in the cockpit, his goggles back, breathing in the cool bracing air and watching the golden fingers of the morning creeping across the blasted landscape far below. It did not seem a day for dying.

Roy Brown was paying no attention to the sun's rays, or anything else about the light or the weather. He was looking over the edge of the cockpit, gazing at the two old De Havillands plodding along some 6,000 feet below. He saw that the trap was perfectly set. All he had to do was spot the German patrol before they spotted him. To Roy Brown it seemed like a perfect day for killing.

It was one of the De Havilland pilots who spotted the Germans first, a cluster of dots to the northeast. He fired a burst of tracers to signal his comrades.

Every man knew that another battle was about to begin.

Gerald Murphy smiled grimly and yanked down his goggles.

Fred Thompson reached forward and cocked his Vickers.

Wop May grinned hugely and buckled the chin-strap of his leather helmet.

The Germans were coming closer. Any second now, Brown knew, they were either going to spot his squadron—or the two scout planes below. The odds were that they would see the De Havillands first, for Brown had kept his squadron on the receding rim of the night's darkness, while the scouts were caught in the dawn.

The Germans took the bait, all right, but they took it too fast, and Roy Brown watched with sudden alarm as the garishly painted planes peeled off into a long screaming descent. As quickly as he could, he threw his own machine into a dive and prayed silently that he, and the others who immediately followed him, could intercept the Germans in time, before they pounced like hawks on the helpless chickens below.

But the bright red Fokker had gotten down within range before Brown could cut him off, and the Canadian saw Richtofen's guns wink as he closed in behind one of the scouts. The De Havilland shuddered, dipped slightly, recovered—and began to smoke. The observer lay slumped in the forward seat, dead, and the pilot tried to claw his way out of the burning plane, while flames licked at his flying suit and reached toward his panic-stricken face.

Richtofen followed behind, enshrouded in the doomed plane's smoke until he bent the Triplane slightly to the left—just in time to see his quarry explode in a bright orange flash and see the pieces of what once was an airplane and two human beings plummet toward the earth.

Richtofen turned away, his face grimly set, and saw a sight that shocked him. Werner Voss was being boxed in by no less than three British planes. Although performing miracles of evasion, he was clearly in bad trouble and needed all the help he could get. Richtofen flipped his plane around and raced toward him.

Above him, Gerald Murphy took the situation in at a glance and saw it as the chance of a lifetime—a chance to revenge himself on Richtofen, to avenge the death of Lanoe Hawker and all the others who had fallen before the bullets of the deadly German. Ripping his leather helmet off with one swipe of his hand, he bore in for the kill, his eyes staring in fixed concentration, his face a mask of hatred and triumph.

And Richtofen was unaware. So concerned was he for Voss' safety that he had momentarily lost interest in everything except coming to his rescue. In doing so, Richtofen opened a chink in his armor that was rare indeed.

He would pay dearly for it.

He was too late to help Voss. Just as Richtofen pulled within firing range, he saw his comrade's plane swoop upward into the converging tracers of two enemy planes, and it was all over. The Halberstadt took several hits and black oil began spewing back across the cockpit; and as Richtofen drew alongside he saw that Voss' head was thrown back and that, unbelievably, the man was roaring with laughter, even as dense smoke began pouring past him in the slipstream. Richtofen knew he was laughing with perverse joy because he had succeeded in choosing his own death and had cheated the rottenness that was consuming his own diseased body from within.

And even as Richtofen watched, Voss squirmed out of the cockpit and put one leg out and then the other, grasping one precarious hand-hold after another until he crouched on the wing of his burning plane. And then, as if a recurrent nightmare was being repeated, Werner Voss glanced around until he saw the blood-red Fokker Triplane flying alongside, fixed his eyes on Richtofen himself, and snapped a jaunty salute that made the baron's bowels turn cold.

And then he dived off into space and began to tumble end over end, just as Oswald Boelcke had done.

In the time it took for all this to happen, Gerald Murphy had closed the gap and the sky behind Richtofen seemed entirely filled with Murphy's Spad. Its guns were slowly shredding the Triplane to ribbons, while Richtofen sat frozen in horror.

Once again, time ran down like a victrola that needs winding, as Richtofen watched the surfaces of his plane slowly disappear, and the fabric and the stringers and the windscreen and everything slowly peeled away. Something hit him a sharp blow on the back of the head knocking him forward.

And when he sat back, his eyes wide-open but seeing nothing, the plane was out of control and spinning earthward. Blood was pouring from under his leather helmet into his eyes. He reached up and wiped the blood away, and blinked a few times until he saw the earth and the sky and the clouds spinning in a vortex of danger that he was at first too groggy to recognize for what it was. It almost seemed to him he could make out the trenches and the roads and the ruined farmhouses, and it was then he realized he was about to die. He roused himself to clutch the control column and put his feet down on the rudder bar and gather the chaos of the crazy spin into one neat package that was a single airplane flying in a single direction.

He was flying parallel to the ground now, only a few feet above that which would kill him if he didn't maintain the hold he had on the balance of the hurtling machine. Before he knew it, he was down and the plane was swapping ends. Richtofen thought his neck had snapped; he could hear the wings cracking off, and the landing gear breaking up. The engine nacelle broke loose from the fuselage, just before the whole fantastic mess that was all that was left of Fokker's creation had finally stopped moving.

As the dust began to settle, the only sound was the distant drone of the battle Richtofen had left behind him and the faint rumble of an artillery barrage many miles distant. Richtofen had crashed near the edge of a small patch of woods in No Man's Land.

Half a mile away, a German officer stood in a trench

and trained his field glasses on the wreck, and saw the Iron Cross insignia on its side.

"Yes," he said aloud. "It's ours—what's left of it."

The grizzled sergeant who stood beside him spoke up. "There's nobody alive in that, sir."

"It doesn't matter, Heinz. We have a standing order. We have no choice."

The sergeant spat angrily into the bottom of the trench. "Damn it, why should we risk—"

"Shut your mouth, Heinz. Get a patrol together and get out to that wreck and see what you can find."

Grudgingly, the veteran sergeant turned and beckoned to the infantrymen down the trench, as the officer took another look through the glasses. He could see a patch of grass burning beside the plane where gasoline had spilled, and . . .

He narrowed his eyes for a closer look. Four or five hundred yards beyond the plane, he thought he saw a blur of movement. As he watched, several figures emerged from the shadows and he recognized them as British soldiers.

"Hurry, Heinz! Tommy's nosing around."

There were eight of them, all wearing the flat dish-helmets and wraparound leggings that made British infantrymen look so clumsy. They were moving directly toward the wrecked plane.

Richtofen was conscious now, just barely. Numbly he watched a leaf falling down from above, scudding and turning and tumbling, reminding him of the way Boelcke fell through the sky, and the way Voss—but no! he would not think about that any more. He would think about the pain only. He would control the pain as he had controlled the plane until the very last moment.

Time was like syrup again, and the leaf was still floating toward him. He watched until it came to rest on his hand, his hand that rested strengthless on the cockpit rim. He raised his hand. The leaf fell away out of sight.

Then he heard a noise close by. Weakly he reached up and drew his shredded helmet off, revealing a gaping, ugly raw wound on one side of his head. He cocked his ear in the direction of the noise.

And then he saw what had made it. A British soldier was approaching the plane, moving toward him like some large brown fish as a wave of pain dealt Richtofen a sickening blow and the world was all under water. He thought he heard a burst of submachine-gun fire nearby and, sure enough, the large brown fish was not moving any more. The pain washed away and Richtofen saw the world as it really was again.

A ruddy face popped over the edge of the cockpit and a pair of frightened but curious eyes peered directly into his; he knew it was another British soldier come to capture him.

The submachine gun barked a second time and the ruddy face was gone; in its place, a pair of hands clutched at the rim of the cockpit, squeezing as if to tear it loose. As the man slumped to the ground and the hands disappeared, Richtofen heard rifle fire close by and shouts of the German rescue patrol as they attacked the British. There were only six of them and they knew they were licked. One of them blew a shrill blast on a policeman's whistle, and they ran for their lives.

Richtofen waited patiently for his rescuers to arrive. The grizzled sergeant walked around the end of the plane to where the baron sat helplessly, and there was a look of curdled bitterness on the sergeant's face that Richtofen couldn't understand—until the sergeant spoke to one of the others.

"It's Richtofen. He cost us Ranier . . . and Paul."

"Never mind that," said the officer. "Get him out of there, and hurry!"

The sun was streaming through the tops of the trees, and Richtofen could see everything that was happening now clearly, for the pain was gone and he was numb.

But as the rescuers leaned over him and prepared to haul him out, he realized that he was seeing everything double.

He blinked his eyes. He still saw everything twice. He fixed his focus on the eyes of the sergeant leaning over him now. It was no use. Blinking didn't help, he was seeing double.

Then, as the sergeant and three others lifted him by the collar and by armpit-holds and by under-the-knee holds, the pain came swamping back and inundated him quickly and efficiently and he passed out with a whimper.

Little painted Prussian soldiers marched in an endless circle around a double-eagle emblem of the Hohenzollern monarchy. When they began to slow down, his mother whirled the tiny merry-go-round again with one finger and held out the spinning toy.

"It's for *you*, little Manfred." She placed it in the toddler's chubby hands.

And the Prussians changed almost imperceptibly into a straight line of boys who were standing in a cobblestoned courtyard in front of a drab gray school building. They all wore ill-fitting cadet uniforms. Little Manfred was one of them, and he took sneaking glances up and down the line, feeling frisky and playful—even though the others were staring stiffly ahead.

A dark shadow loomed over him and he looked up, smiling, at the school commandant.

"And who are you, young sir?"

"I'm Manfred, sir."

The commandant bellowed down at him in an outraged manner. *"Manfred?* There is no *Manfred* here."

The boy's face fell.

"You are von Richtofen, do you understand? You are Richtofen!"

Now the boy stood straight like the others, staring stiffly ahead, and the line of cadets changed almost imperceptibly once again into a line of splendidly uniformed Prussian soldiers who began to march in a wide circle, and once again the miniature merry-go-round was whirling.

Manfred von Richtofen awoke slowly in the hospital bed, his eyelids fluttering a few moments until he was fully conscious. What he saw directly before him, like a vision, was the loveliest face he had ever seen. And when he saw the white cap on the back of her dark hair he knew instantly where he was. The young nurse was smiling tenderly down at him, as if she had known him, and loved him, all her life. Richtofen wondered if he were delirious.

"Herr Rittmeister," she murmured softly. "At last you are awake."

Richtofen tried to gather himself to sit up, but she put out a hand and held him back.

He struggled to speak. "I—I am . . ."

"You have come through the worst," she said. "The fever's broken and you're through the worst. I'll call the doctor."

She made a move to rise, but Richtofen reached out weakly and clutched at her hand. She gazed down at him with a look of such sweetness that Richtofen could almost feel his heart melt.

"Nurse . . . you've been with me since . . . since I came?"

They were holding hands now. "I've always been here," she told him softly.

And then the young nurse became embarrassed. "Did—did you sleep well?" she asked nervously.

"I dreamed," said Richtofen, remembering the miniature merry-go-round and the school commandant. "I never used to dream at all."

The young nurse smiled. "It doesn't mean anything. The crash was very violent. You received a concussion. Sometimes . . ."

The young baron smiled. "So crashes make one dream, do they?"

She answered him very seriously, like a schoolmistress getting across a point to a child. "A severe insult to the brain—"

"Like war?" Richtofen cut in.

But she didn't smile at his little ironic sally, and he saw that she took him very seriously.

She was staring down at him, her blue eyes gleaming with admiration.

"They say you were very brave."

The baron started to laugh, but his head hurt terribly and his hand went quickly to the bandage that covered one side above his ear.

"Brave? Because I stayed with the plane? Hell, they don't give us parachutes. That makes us very brave indeed."

But she still wouldn't smile.

"If there's anything . . ." she said, shyly.

"I'm sure there will be something," Richtofen said teasingly, and watched her blush.

She rose abruptly and started out of the room, and he stopped her with his voice. "There *is* one thing . . ."

She stopped at the door and turned.

"Your name."

"Katie," she said. "Katie Odersdorf."

"Thank you," he said, still teasing her. "I'm Richtofen."

"I know."

And she disappeared in a whirl of white skirts.

Wind Commander Owen couldn't believe his ears. He stood up behind his desk and looked into their hard young faces.

"You wish to—to *raid the German aerodrome?*"

Roy Brown grinned wolfishly. "Around five-thirty or six in the evening, sir."

Wing Commander Owen looked disgusted. "That's about at supper time, if I'm not mistaken."

Fred Thompson laughed coarsely. The others waited in guarded silence.

That's the hour, sir," agreed Roy Brown. "Around supper time."

"Well, Commander?" asked Wop May.

Owen shook his head. "I have to think about it, gentlemen." And he looked at Brown sternly. "I can't help wondering what Major—"

"Hawker's dead, sir," said Gerald Murphy.

"Quite right," said Owen, glaring at Brown. "Sometimes I . . . forget."

Chapter 12

Richtofen had been home on convalescent leave now for several days. Most of that time had been spent hunting, an old love of his, for the woods and meadows and streams of the Richtofen estate in Silesia were fairly teeming with game of all kinds. It was on this estate, during his boyhood years, that Richtofen had learned the mysteries of the hunt—a background that came in handy in the skies over France.

One bright afternoon he strode up to the front door of the Richtofen mansion with a string of hares over his shoulder. Every afternoon he had come in with something. As usual, one of the servants came out to meet him and the young baron handed the game to him. Richtofen entered the house and strode through the great high-ceilinged rooms until he came to the garden terrace where his mother and Kate Odersdorf were having their usual afternoon tea.

"Was there anything stirring out there, Manfred?" his mother asked.

"A few hares. Nothing much."

A servant appeared with a steaming cup of tea and handed it carefully to the young baron.

"Herr Pasenau came by this afternoon," said his mother.

"Oh?"

"He said there's a boar pestering his corn. I said I'd mention it to you."

"Perhaps I'll find the time to hunt it for him. Perhaps not." He sipped his tea and thought back in time. "How long do you suppose it's been since I—"

"It was June, nineteen thirteen," said his mother.

Richtofen stared at her, amazed. "I beg your pardon?"

"Your last boar, my dear." She laughed to herself. "Lothar said you handled him clumsily—but of course you denied it."

"My God, how do you manage it? How do you remember?"

"I remember whatever has to do with my sons. Whatever matters to them matters to me."

Richtofen was moved by her simple statement of devotion. He put his cup down and leaned toward her. "It's been a long time since we had a good talk, hasn't it, Mother? I want to know about the things that really matter to you."

She reached out slowly and touched the bandage that still hid the wound from sight.

"My sons," she said. "That's what really matters to me."

Kate Odersdorf, sitting quietly facing them, felt the tears come into her eyes.

"And now," said the older woman, changing the mood gracefully if abruptly, "I think it must be time for our lovely guest to see to your bandage. What do you think, my dear girl?"

The young woman smiled and rose from her chair.

"I think that would be a good idea, Frau Richtofen."

"You two run along, then. I want to read my paper."

Manfred rose, and the two of them disappeared inside the house; Frau Richtofen smiled after them.

Richtofen was sitting on the edge of the bed, stripped to the waist. His head was free of the bandage now, and the ugly red wound gaped shockingly above his left ear. The hair on either side of the wound had been shaved away, making the long furrow all the more conspicuous. Kate Odersdorf sat beside him, cleaning the edges of the wound with an alcohol-soaked pad. Occasionally she touched him with her free hand, pretending to steady herself as she worked, but really caressing him on the arm, on the shoulder, on the back of his neck.

Richtofen did not appear to notice any of this, either the cleansing of his wound or the way she caressed his body. He was gazing intently toward the window, in a fixed stare broken only by an occasional hard blink.

"It's looking much better now," said Kate Odersdorf. "How does it feel?"

But Richtofen didn't answer. The young nurse put her hands in her lap and watched him closely. "It was kind of you to arrange for me to attend you."

Richtofen closed his eyes and opened them again. Was he simply ignoring her?

"I didn't mean to bore you," she said, her voice not as soft as before.

Richtofen turned and looked at her. "What? Oh, I'm sorry, Katie. It's . . . I seem to have a headache."

Quickly she rose from the edge of the bed and stood directly in front of him, frowning with concern. "Where? Where's the pain?"

Richtofen looked at the carpet, not wanting to reveal what he had seen.

"Does it hurt around the wound?"

Resolutely he raised his eyes to her, and hoped he wouldn't see the same thing again. But as he focused on her face, the image blurred, then split into a perfect double-image. Everything he had looked at during the past two minutes had gone double.

"Please tell me," she pleaded.

He smiled sardonically. "There seem to be two of you, Katie. Both very lovely . . . but, two of you."

She kneeled in front of him and cupped his face in her hands, and as she came ever closer the images fused at last into one.

He reached out and pulled her into his arms, and kissed her. And when it was over he spoke lightly. "It's nothing, really. I think it was only a trick of the light."

That settled, he pulled her up on the bed. And she did not resist. But she did look worried as he began to kiss her neck, her shoulders, her—

"What if someone should come in?" she asked, alarmed in a way that charmed him to the core.

"Don't be ridiculous, Katie," he said, teasing her with mock severity. "No one would enter without permission. There's such a thing as decent conduct, you know!"

To the startled German guard at the gate, the world was filled with nothing but noise, a steadily increasing drone that seemed to come from all directions at once. At the very last moment he caught sight of the low-level formation just above the tree tops to the west. One of them was slanting down slightly more than the others and heading straight at him, but before he could lift his rifle and shoot at the monster he saw the machine guns flicker, and simultaneously was thrown backward onto the ground like a bundle of bloody rags. The formation passed directly overhead.

Some of the German pilots had been sitting in the wardroom when the sound of the approaching formation first had been heard. The older ones among them, recognizing what was happening, immediately ran outside, pulling on their flying jackets as they ran. A line of dust spurts ripped through them as the first slanting Sopwith Camel let loose the second burst of the battle, and several German pilots joined the sentry in death.

Several others were sitting in the messhall when the attack began, oblivious to the oncoming drone. Only at the last minute, when it was too late, did some of them rise from their seats and move toward the exit, but the wall behind them suddenly dissolved in an imploding wave of plaster and board and ear-shattering noise. One officer was hurled backward in the air, sprawling the entire length of the long mess-table, sliding to a stop at the end so that his head flopped backward over the end and the blood poured in gushes from his mouth.

Lieutenant Lothar von Richtofen was the only German pilot to reach his plane. Ernst Udet was racing toward his when he saw it explode, and without hesitation he turned and stopped to help Lothar.

"Do you have ammunition?" he shouted at Lothar, already strapped in.

"How the hell do I know? Just get out there and start my motor!"

Udet ran to the front of the plane, spun the propeller with one mighty burst of energy, and the engine caught at once. Udet busied himself yanking the chocks from the two wheels and, almost before he had time to get out of the way, the plane was taxiing ahead. As Lothar began to pick up speed, he was spotted from the air. It was Fred Thompson who saw him.

Lothar sat hunched as low as he could in the cockpit, paying no attention to the bomb burst off to his right as one of the hangars was obliterated, gunning his straining engine for all it was worth. And just as the plane lifted off, Thompson came roaring down on him and the runway ahead was slashed with two rows of tracer-trails. Lothar saw that there was no escape: unless the English pilot took his finger off the trigger, Lothar's machine was going to fly into the killing zone of the fire.

And so it was.

His face curdled in agony as a bullet drilled through his right leg and wood struts and canvas were blasted away all around him.

The plane, several feet off the ground, wobbled like a stricken eagle, began to pour smoke, and started to fall off on its left wing. When it touched ground at the end of the runway, Lothar was unable to keep it straightened out and everything went to hell in a violent ground loop that sent the plane crashing into the woods.

Several hundred yards away, at the head of the runway, Ernst Udet stood stock-still and watched as the plane exploded in the trees and was obscured in a pall of black smoke.

Udet began to run. It seemed to take him forever to reach the spot where Lothar lay. Between the time Udet started and the time he arrived, Lothar Richtofen had lived a lifetime of terror.

For Lothar had been thrown clear of the wreck and, fearing the flames, had pulled his pain-wracked body erect and tried to move away. But his leg collapsed under him and he yelled from the pain of it and froze in position, fearing to move again lest the searing pain destroy him. Glancing back down the runway he saw the flashes of exploding bombs, the fires of the burning planes and hangars, and the figure of Udet running toward him. Out of the welter of confusing sounds, one single steady drone emerged, distinct and deadly, and Lothar glanced up to see the same British plane that had shot him down now boring in on him again.

Thompson's plane flattened out into a strafing run and Lothar was moving before the first burst of tracer-fire lanced out in his direction, limping in a series of agonizing movements toward the nearest tree and making it just in time, as the bark on one side of it was turned into splinters and wood-powder and chunks of kindling.

And suddenly it was all over. The British planes were gone.

Udet came crashing through the underbrush and knelt down beside him. "Where are you hit?"

Lothar was shaking all over from the pain and the

fright. "God knows," he said. "All I know is, I feel like a gutted animal, as if every bone in my body were broken."

Udet lit a cigaret for him and inserted it between his lips.

"What's it like back there?" asked Lothar, indicating with a nod of his head the main part of the aerodrome.

"It's hell. They've wrecked every plane on the flight line. Nobody got off the ground. They blew up the messhall, the barracks, the fuel dump, *everything*!"

Udet had ripped off part of his jacket and was busy putting a tourniquet on Lothar's right leg, where the worst bleeding was. Lothar saw that Udet was shaking too.

"Haven't you ever seen men killed before?" he asked.

"Not like this," said Udet. "It's like the trenches."

Lothar cried out in pain as Udet cinched the cloth tightly. "They—they brought the trenches to us," he said, groaning. "Do you see, Udet?"

"See what?"

"Goering's right ... he's right!" Then he lay back, exhausted, and added quietly, "The old way doesn't make sense any more."

"I see you're feeling much better, my boy."

Manfred nodded. He and his father each sat astride a stallion, riding slowly along a wooded trail.

"And I'm very glad of it," the older man continued. "There's so much left to do. We have to end this war."

Richtofen smiled and glanced over at him. "That would be a fine thing," he said.

"When this is over, we'll put things back to rights. We'll use the army to clean out the socialist rabble."

They were approaching the outskirts of a small village. Some of the poor folk of the town stopped to stare at the two gentlemen passing by. Manfred noticed the raw sullenness of their expressions. It saddened him to realize how little his aristocratic father understood of the present conditions. Perhaps it was just as well, Manfred thought to himself. It would cause him too much pain to learn that the old order had passed away.

"Workers' parties," the old gentleman was saying, with a sneer in his voice. "Peasants presuming to make policy. This war will put an end to all that. Things will be different when it's all over."

"They will indeed, Father. They will indeed."

The elder Richtofen nodded sharply, glumly, glad that his son was agreeing with him, not knowing that Manfred was only being diplomatic.

Later that afternoon, they talked in the study, and once again Manfred was struck with his father's naiveté. The old man stood before the fireplace, holding an ancient, leather-bound book with brass clasps, and his eyes had a faraway look. "I was reading this last night. It's a history of Frederick the Second, the Holy Roman Emperor. His son, Manfred, was a Teutonic knight."

Manfred von Richtofen took a sip of sherry and spoke with mild sarcasm. "A great hero."

And his father turned and smiled at him. "I named you after him."

Manfred took his glass over to the huge window on the far side of the study and stared out at the lovely, late-afternoon scene of stately trees and broad grassy meadows, with a blue canopy of sky above it all. "I wonder if that Manfred enjoyed the sun," he said reflectively. "One should . . ."

But the elder Richtofen was dwelling in the musty halls of history and did not hear what his son had said. "In Italy, you know, he fought against great odds."

And Manfred, lost in the present as his father was lost in the past, did not hear what the elder Richtofen had said. The two men were simply talking, each as if the other were not in the room. "Do you suppose he liked dogs and hunting?"

"An immortal . . ."

Manfred did hear that, and responded to it. "An immortal who died, and was buried on the field."

". . . to live forever with the heroes of the Fatherland."

"To be disinterred by his enemies," Manfred added savagely, "his bones left to bleach on the banks of a river."

But his father did not hear, and kept on in his reverie.

Manfred gulped the rest of the sherry. He knew it was hopeless. His father was going to have to learn the hard way that the world had taken a radical turn since he last looked out from the moated castle that was his mind.

What the hell does it matter? he asked himself bitterly. *All I want to do is get back and erase more British planes from the sky.*

Chapter 13

"Lovely, that's what it was!" shouted Gerald Murphy.

He and the others, still wearing their flying gear, sat around the round table in Operations with coffee cups in their hands.

"Their whole bloody safe sweet world going up in flames," said Fred Thompson. "It was—"

"—bloody lovely," said Wop May.

An officer from Intelligence, dapper in a freshly pressed uniform, sat among them calmly puffing on his pipe. He was totally unmoved by their excitement.

"Lieutenant," he said, turning to Roy Brown. "Have you any count on aircraft destroyed?"

"Anywhere from fifteen to twenty. It's hard to say precisely. Everything visible was smashed."

The Intelligence man scribbled notes in his pad. "Fine. And what about personnel?"

"I beg your pardon?"

Thompson cut in. "He means, how many of the bastards did we kill. We killed plenty. They were still in the mess-hall. You see—we thought if we hit them right at suppertime, why, it would be—"

"—it would be what you might call the last supper," said Gerald Murphy.

The other pilots exploded into raucous guffaws. The Intelligence man looked from one face to another, wondering what made pilots so frivolous. Wing Commander Owen had come into the room just in time to hear Murphy's irreverant remark. His lined, weary face registered the disgust he felt.

"You destroyed the ammunition shed and hit the officers' mess," the Intelligence officer went on. "What about the barracks?"

Thompson frowned, pondering, then looked over at Wop May. "May, you were the one that hit that long brown building, weren't you?"

"Yes—you suppose that was the barracks? Why, I'll bet it *was*."

The Intelligence man was scribbling again. He didn't look up as he said, "No, that was the hospital."

And there was a loud silence. The wing commander stared at the dapper officer in horror.

"Am I to understand that my people bombed—a *hospital*?"

The Intelligence man glanced up quizzically. All he wanted was the facts, and he wasn't interested in any display of emotion. He turned to Wop May. "Did you see a Red Cross flag in front of the building, or on top of it?"

May squirmed uncomfortably. "It—it was twilight, you know. I didn't see anything."

"Ah, then it couldn't have been a hospital, could it," said the officer, smiling to himself, closing the matter.

Whether it was a hospital or not really didn't matter to him in the least.

"Just a moment, Major," said Owen, obviously very angry. "Are you trying to tell me that the placement of a Red Cross flag is what determines whether a building is a hospital or not?"

The Intelligence man, seeing that the commander wasn't going to let the matter pass so easily, fell back on technicalities. "The Hague Convention makes it clear that in the absence of such markings—"

But Owen cut him off rudely. "Would the presence of wounded men, doctors, and nurses have anything bearing on your classification?"

The officer seemed puzzled by the question. "Essentially, no."

Roy Brown had been listening closely, saying nothing. Now he lit a cigaret and watched the flame consume the match until it was a crumpled black char between his fingers. Any doubts he had had in the past were now dispelled. This major from Intelligence had the same point of view toward the war that he had. What the man said next confirmed it.

"Commander," said the major, speaking slowly, as if to a retarded child, "I'm afraid the cricket match is over and done with. It's an entirely new kind of war. In the next few weeks you'll be receiving detailed orders for antipersonnel raids all along this front. Strafing attacks, ambushes of officer personnel, destruction of all kinds of supplies, including medical."

The wing commander looked very old and very drawn. "Are there any limits left, Major?"

"We didn't initiate this raising of the stakes. They've begun to strafe our pilots on the ground."

"You mean that incident at Le Hamel? That single incident opened all this up?"

"I'm afraid I don't know the incident you're speaking of. We've got at least fifty separate and solidly documented cases on file. This kind of thing is happening all across the Western Front."

As the pilots and the major from Intelligence coldly watched him, Owen turned and left the room.

Roy Brown smiled to himself. There would be no more interference from that quarter.

They were lying side-by-side in Richtofen's room. In the corner a red-shaded lamp shed a dim glow.

"What will you do when I go back?" he asked.

"Do? Why, I'll return to the hospital."

He took a slow puff from the long Turkish cigar he held in one hand. They lay there, looking at the ceiling.

"My God," said Kate suddenly, laughing, "you should have heard the others when they found I'd been assigned to you. There wasn't a single nurse who wouldn't have given her soul for—for a night like this."

He drew on his cigar again, then squinted at its burning end. "How absurd. They don't even know me."

"Of course they know you. Everyone in the world knows you. And they—the other nurses, I mean—they *wanted* you."

Richtofen turned his head slightly and looked at her. "Wanted me?"

"To be with you, like this. They'll never *be* anything, don't you see? Wife of a Munich butcher, a Leipzig electrician—if any butchers and electricians survive this war."

"So why me? They'd do better with the electrician."

Kate smiled wickedly at him. "Oh, it's not that they want you *forever*. But everyone wants something to remember. One night would be enough. Do you see?"

Richtofen saw, and was embarrassed. Rather gruffly he sat up with the cigar between his teeth. "It's time. The car will be here soon."

He dressed quickly, without a word, as she lay there watching him. When he was finished he stood before the mirror, and cocked his cap until it was just the way he wanted it. He glanced at Kate's reflection—and saw a double image.

Whirling, he focussed his eyes on her, glaring hard. The double-image was gone, and he relaxed and enjoyed what was to be his last look at Katie Odersdorf. It took him several seconds, for she was as nearly naked as a woman can be with only one corner of a sheet to cover her. She smiled at him, utterly desirable.

"If—when you come back—if you want to reach me . . ."

Richtofen smiled without humor and wrenched his eyes away from her. "Reach you? I thought I had."

He ground out the cigar in an ashtray atop the bureau. And walked out. Kate watched the last vague ghost of smoke dispel, and only then allowed herself to cry.

It was dawn when Richtofen reached the end of his

journey. Great rolling clouds of morning mist were rolling slowly across the landscape, and the driver steered the car with care and caution.

At the aerodrome, the clean-up crews were just finishing their gruesome task of collecting the corpses from the British air raid. Flickering fires from the still-smouldering buildings cast an eerie glow in the rolling mist, and the workers moved in and out of it like wraiths. The corpses had been lined up at the northern edge of the flying field, their pale faces toward the sky, still and shapeless as puppets. At the end lay the body of a young nurse, her head shattered like a broken egg, her eyes wide open as if in a terrible kind of astonishment. One of the workers, an infantryman like the rest, was struggling nearby with a heavy beam that was covering what looked like still another body.

"Did you see that girl?" he asked his helper, another infantryman. "The one over on the bone-pile?"

And the other man, grunting against the stubborn beam, said, "If I'd been here she'd still be alive."

"What d'ya mean, Fritz?"

"Why, I'd have covered her with my own body, if you know what I mean!"

They laughed coarsely and, with a final effort, succeeded in pushing the beam aside. Sure enough, there was a corpse underneath, mangled and all mashed up with other debris. Roughly they reached down together, peeled it free and tossed it aside heavily, and began to dig for others.

A motor car pulled up nearby and they turned to look. They did not recognize Baron Manfred von Richtofen as he opened the rear door and stepped out. The two soldiers went back to their digging.

Richtofen looked around him, utterly bewildered. His eye fell on the line of corpses and then the nurse at the end. He thought of Kate, and went over to where the body lay. Reverently he knelt down and placed his cloak over the terrible face, then rose to his feet again.

"Rittmeister!"

It was Max Holzapfel. His face was lined with dirt and he looked bone-weary.

"Holzapfel—what *happened*?"

"Thank God you're back, Herr Rittmeister. The British, they did this. Things are going to hell all about us. Not only the raid, but the Americans now. More planes from the Americans as well."

Richtofen grabbed the older man by the shoulders. "Get hold of yourself, Holzapfel."

The crewman shook his head in shock.

"Lothar!" said Richtofen. "Where's my brother?"

"He survived, but it was a miracle. They strafed him as he tried to get into the air. They shot him off the runway and then strafed him as he ran into the woods— like a rat in a basket. The bastards!"

"Holzapfel, is he—"

"He's alive. Only a leg wound and a few bruises. You'll find him in the aid tent, over there." He pointed to a row of tents between the road and the woods. "Shall I take you to him, sir?"

"Later. Right now we have a squadron to put back together. What do we have left? What can you patch together?"

The crewman stared at him, dazed and unbelieving.

"You mean—*planes*? Sir, look around you! It would take two days just to find parts enough to cannibalize. There's nothing."

But Richtofen was hardly listening. Instead he was trying to figure out how to perform a miracle, and his mind was racing.

"Where the hell is Werner?" he asked suddenly.

Holzapfel looked puzzled. "I don't understand, sir."

"Voss—where is Voss? I need him now."

The dirt-streaked crewman reached out and gently took hold of his superior's arm. He saw that Richtofen had broken out in a cold sweat, as if he had malaria.

"Herr Rittmeister. Lieutenant Voss is dead. He fell the same day you were shot down."

Richtofen, deeply embarrassed over what he considered a moment of weakness, tried to cover it up with a gruff response. "Yes, of course—I remember."

And he remembered too well, as Werner Voss was resurrected briefly in his mind's eye, tumbling downward through the battle-loud sky.

As Richtofen began to walk slowly toward the temporary operations center—an open-sided tent—the tired crewman followed behind, concern showing in his face. The surviving pilots saw him coming and gathered quickly, Udet shaping them into a rough formation to greet their squadron leader. But Udet failed to call them to attention, and they were free to cheer. They did, as loud as they were able.

When they saw Richtofen's expression, however, the cheer died away.

"Plenty of time for emotion later, gentlemen," said the baron, stopping stiffly before them. "Right now I want status reports from every officer. I do *not* want hysterical surmise. I want to know if there are any planes we can fly. I want to know what our casualties are. I want to know how soon we can expect replacements."

All through his staccato-style speech, the sound of motors had been growing in volume. Richtofen noticed that, at first, the men glanced nervously at the sky to the west, as if they feared another air attack. The sound of the motors nearly drowned his words, and he turned irritably to see what it was.

A convoy of trucks was approaching, a dust trail following them far down the road. Richtofen and the others watched as the lead truck turned onto the aerodrome access road and led the convoy straight across to the tents. The lead truck came to a halt, the others braking behind. A heavy-set, scowling sergeant climbed down to the ground and dusted himself off.

"Who's in charge here?" he bellowed. No one answered him. "Damn it, I haven't got all day."

He came stomping over to where Richtofen stood, saw the baron's shoulder insignia, and stiffened into a smart salute.

"I am Richtofen. What have you brought?"

The sergeant was very talkative. "What have I brought? Well, sir, I have a baker's dozen of airplanes, is what I have. Twelve ordinary planes, and one other besides them that isn't ordinary at all."

"Go on."

"Well, sir, it's the damnedest looking three-winged machine you ever saw."

The pilots looked at each other in astonishment, and

Ernst Udet stepped forward to clutch Richtofen's sleeve. "It's Fokker's planes! He wired us awhile back to say we could expect them any day now."

Richtofen's smile was beatific. In the twinkling of an eye he had changed from a stunned squadron leader, trying to put a chaotic situation straight again, to a man whose greatest passion in life was to hunt. Standing off to one side, Max Holzapfel noted the abrupt transition with fascination.

"All right," shouted Richtofen, his body vibrating with excitement, "let's get them uncrated and assembled. Every one of us will have to do the work of three men—if you expect to raid the British this evening . . ."

The pilots gawked at him.

"That's what I said, gentlemen. *This evening.*"

Without a further word, they all began to race toward the trucks.

In the few hours since their spectacular raid on the enemy aerodrome, the British pilots had ridden the crest of a wave of savage joy, for their warrior calling had been fulfilled in spades. Even their recreation had become savage in a way. Roy Brown and Wop May had organized a no-holds-barred rugby match, and those pilots and crewmen bold enough to join in were astonished at the pace the two Canadians set and even more astonished at the brutal but high-spirited violence of the game.

Dozens of men stood or sat on the sidelines, drinking deeply from large mugs of beer and cheering the players on. Behind them, on the other side where the

Sopwith Camels were arrayed on the flight line, the rest of the pilots and staff and a few visitors were having a time of it dancing with some nurses from a field hospital, swinging across the grass to the music of an orchestra of French civilians and British soldiers.

And beyond that, the soft wind of springtime France made the tall grass in the pastures wave like the sea, and a herd of cows grazed peacefully. Along one edge of the nearest pasture, a laughing young pilot ran after a gaily screeching nurse, she zigging, he zagging, until they finally bumped into one another and went down in the tall grass and realized they were alone and apart from the rest of the crowd.

On this brilliant spring afternoon, only Wing Commander Owen and the soldiers of the guard remained aloof from the festivities. Owen stood with his arms crossed watching the rugby match, glancing at his watch every few minutes, conscious that it would soon be time to lower the flag that was flapping in the warm breeze behind him.

Roy Brown and Wop May, sweat dripping from their hair, staggered off the field and over to the enormous beer keg where a crewman was passing out foaming glasses. Taking their mugs with them, the two Canadians wandered over to the nearest tree and slumped down against it, and guzzled their beer.

"I just can't get over it, Roy. We didn't even lose a single plane. We didn't have one single solitary casualty!"

Brown nodded abstractly. "You know, I really think we can break them. By sheer relentlessness. Right now, we probably have them wiped out as far as operational aircraft goes. It'll be weeks before they're in shape to launch a serious combat patrol."

May took another swig and wiped foam off his lips. "You don't seem exactly overjoyed about it."

"Me? Hell, I'm glad enough. It's only that I . . ."

"Yes?"

"I just thought it would be easier, more bearable, somehow, if we chucked all the damned gentlemanly nonsense and got on with the job."

"You were so right, Roy."

In the distance could be heard the droning of a large number of planes, still far enough away that the two men ignored it.

"And yet," Brown continued, "I can't help wondering if Major Hawker didn't know something, something I had never thought of until now."

Wop May frowned and put his mug carefully down on the grass. "What, Roy? What did Hawker know?"

Brown finished his beer and got to his feet, May following, and the two men strolled casually down the runway.

The sound of the oncoming planes grew louder, still not loud enough to drown the strains from the accordian over where the dancing was.

"Maybe he knew that we *have* to pretend that our warfare is decent and honorable and righteous—or go mad."

May laughed uncertainly. "Pretending is for children."

They were nearing the end of the runway, and the great droning filled the air.

"I think you've been at it too long, Roy. Your ulcers

show it, and your fatigue. And anyway, this isn't a philosophical matter. Not really."

"Who said it was?"

"I'll tell you what it *is,* though. It's nothing but a problem in applied physics. That's all war is, actually."

They halted at the end of the runway.

"I guess that's a reasonable way of looking at it," said Brown, wanting desperately to agree. "A problem in applied physics . . ."

Only then did they turn to see what the noise was.

Over where the dancing was, the orchestra was beginning to falter, as the musicians looked up at the sky. The rugby players paused.

Over by Operations, two members of the guard were lowering the flag. Wing Commander Owen stood by, frozen in a regulation salute to the flag.

There were thirteen German planes. One was slightly ahead of the others. They were flying daringly close to the ground, no more than thirty feet in the air. And as Brown and May watched, the guns of the plane in front winked briefly and the turf all around them exploded in jets of dust and pebbles. The two men dived for the ground and instinctively tried to bury themselves under the turf.

The burst ended and a blood-red DR-1 Triplane zoomed overhead.

Richtofen's second burst ripped the rear fuselage stringers out of two Camels on the flight line and turned the top wing of a third into a useless sagging of canvas and wood.

The two guards at the flagpole were like statues now

and the Union Jack hung flapping at half-mast. Wing
Commander Owen held his salute stubbornly.

"Get on with it, men!" he shouted.

But the guards broke and ran, their faces white with
fear as the planes kept coming and other machine guns
opened up. And Richtofen, about to pull back on the
control column, caught a split-second glimpse of a lone
Englishman reaching up to gather a flag in his arms and
gave his Spandaus a third workout. And even as the
blood-red Fokker banked around for another run,
Wing Commander Owen lay in a spreading pool of his
own blood.

But Richtofen had already forgotten the image and
didn't care whether he had hit the man or not. What he
wanted now was to hit more men, to destroy life, to
tear up everything he saw below—the planes, the buildings, and the tiny ant-like creatures that were racing
frantically in all directions as he came in for his second
strafing run.

At the edge of the pasture, just before the end of
the runway, he saw two figures lying in the grass. The
one on the bottom was dressed in white, and even before he realized it was a nurse, and a soldier trying to
protect her, Richtofen turned them both into bags of
blood with one squeeze of his trigger.

And kept his finger on the trigger, and watched the
tracers lance out across an open place with a platform
with chairs on it, and men and women pressing themselves against the ground and a big wooden tub that
broke apart in the rain of bullets and gushed foaming
beer all over the grass, splashing the people who had
fallen nearby.

And kept his finger on the trigger still and once again saw the flagpole, and his tracers splintered it and riddled the Union Jack until the whole assembly fell to the ground.

If Baron Manfred von Richtofen had somehow been able to see himself he would have suffered a terrible shock, for his handsome face was frozen in a facial contortion that made him look like Satan himself.

Richtofen, the first into the attack, was the first to break off. As he soared upward into the clouds, heading toward the formation's rendezvous point, he didn't bother to look back. He knew the score had been evened, for during his third run he had seen out of the corner of his eye the damage his comrades had already caused in their initial run, as debris from planes lay scattered all over the runway and several buildings were going up in flames.

Down below, it was suddenly deafeningly quiet. The drone of the German planes had receded entirely and now, for one moment, there was no sound at all. And then a cry of pain was heard, and a groan, and in the lengthening twilight shadows the figures of those who survived began to appear amid the smoke and flame. Men and woman staggered aimlessly about, stunned and bewildered.

Out at the ends of the runway, two men slowly sat up and gazed at the panorama of smashed Camels and the inferno of the buildings beside the field. An oil-drum fire sent a pillar of black smoke high into the darkening sky.

"My God," murmured Wop May. "My God. How could they do it? How did they manage?"

Roy Brown shook his head in disbelief. "We—we thought they were crippled, but we made a mistake, didn't we?"

Brown climbed painfully to his feet and May followed suit, and they stood there in the lowering rays of the blinding red sunset.

"No, that's wrong," said Brown decisively. "It wasn't a mistake. It was a miscalculation—" He turned toward May—"like you might make in physics."

Chapter 14

The end was coming. Everyone knew it. Now that the Americans were in the war, it was obvious it could not last much longer.

As the bitter weeks sped by, Baron von Richtofen continued to win battle after battle in the sky until his total score stood near eighty. But he knew that winning battles did not necessarily mean winning wars; he knew, as well as the next man, that this war was already a lost cause. Even so, he put it out of his mind. As always, Baron Manfred von Richtofen was a soldier first and foremost; he intended to perform his soldierly duties with single-minded determination until such day as he could no longer fly a plane, or until such day as the war was declared over, or until such day as he was dead.

One by one he had watched his comrades-in-arms go down in flames. Udet and Goering remained. Lothar remained. All the others were gone, and he barely knew the new men. There was no time for socializing. Whatever warmth he was able to display in the past was gone now and his men, even his brother, left him alone with his ice-cold thoughts of duty and honor and the destruction of the enemy.

One day he was called to a meeting in the officers' mess-hall. When he arrived he was greeted warmly by von Hoeppner, who was a general now. There were others present.

"Sit down, Richtofen," he said heartily, indicating a chair at the opposite end of the long table. "This may be one of the most important meetings you'll ever attend."

When he had taken his seat, Richtofen glanced around and was surprised to see that Anthony Fokker was present, along with some Air Service officers. Richtofen and the suave plane designer exchanged silent greetings, just as the meeting was called to order by General von Hoeppner.

"Major Trackl, we will hear your report now," said the general.

A lean young officer rose and looked around from face to face. He wore his hair very short, and when he spoke it was with a clipped, military delivery that Richtofen would have found almost humorous—if it were not so sinister.

"Gentlemen, the current Intelligence picture of our situation is—*bleak,* to say the least. Within six to eight months a general Allied offensive, strengthened by the new American divisions, will commence. It is clear to Intelligence that the offensive will be—terminal."

Trackl paused, expecting a token protest or two, but no one said a word.

"We will not be able to resist it," he continued in a matter-of-fact tone. "We shall be pushed beyond the

Rhine within four months. The enemy will invade the Reich immediately thereafter."

"All right, Major," said von Hoeppner. "You may sit down." He looked around the room and said: "Gentlemen, you will notice that no notes are being taken of this meeting. That is because this meeting is, in an official sense, not taking place. I trust you understand. Your discretion is absolutely essential."

Next he called on a tall, powerfully built colonel whom Richtofen had never seen before, and the man rose.

"Gentlemen, the Empire is finished. Even if the Allies do not insist on the establishment of a republican government, internal pressures will bring this into being—"

"Explain to these gentlemen what you mean by 'internal pressures,'" said Hoeppner.

"I am referring to those elements in our society aligning themselves with the Communists, such as the Left Unions and the Spartakist League, as well as the general unrest and turmoil brought on by food shortages and so on."

"Go on, then."

"To continue: if we are forced to an armistice, the possibilities run between an orderly formation of a republic that will be supported by the Allies, leading to a viable unity among the German people, or a Bolshevik regime founded on class hatred, erected in mass bloodshed, and controlled by Moscow."

Quietly from the far end of the table Richtofen spoke. "Gentlemen, am I to understand that this is a revolutionary council?"

Although he asked the question in a deceptively bland manner, everyone saw the fire in his eyes. The young major named Trackl burst out passionately.

"Damn it, Richtofen, they've lost the war. It's over—except the killing and dying. We're ruined, but no one at the top is willing to admit it. If there's going to be a Fatherland of the future, someone must make a move—*now*."

The tall colonel nodded, and added: "We have to plan, for next time . . ."

"And *next* time," said Trackl, shaking his clenched fist in the air, "the Jews and the Communists and the merchants won't have a chance to sell us—"

General von Hoeppner suddenly rapped the table with his knuckles. "That's enough. Herr Richtofen, we came here to speak with you about Germany's future, and to explain to you why I am removing you from the flying roster."

Richtofen was sitting low in his chair, his hands clasped calmly beneath his chin. His face was inscrutable now. Everyone waited for him to respond to this news, but there was no response.

"You do understand the reasons for this move, I trust," continued Hoeppner, keeping his gaze on the baron. "It is imperative that we retain a nucleus of the finest of our armed forces."

"Of course the General Staff itself will be kept intact," said the big colonel.

"Officers will be hired by various industries," said Trackl. "Sections will be kept together secretly."

They were trying very hard to win Richtofen over to their way of thinking, but no one yet knew his thoughts on the matter. Now Anthony Fokker added his voice to the chorus of persuasion.

"You would become the Fokker Company's chief test pilot, if you wished. In addition to our commercial contracts, we will be producing designs suitable for modification to military use. We will design a series of racing planes, you see, that would . . ."

And here his voice trailed off, for he could plainly see in Richtofen's eyes the profound contempt that was there.

Richtofen slowly pushed back his chair and rose.

"I'm valuable to you, am I?" He shook his head, an ironic smirk twisting his lips. "You *order* me to grounded status. And then you tell me to save myself for the glorious future—"

"Mind your manners, Richtofen," said the general. "We came to speak to you an an equal. We have given you no cause to—"

"An equal?" said Richtofen, and his voice was openly contemptuous. "I am not your equal. Or perhaps I should say you are not *my* equal. For I am a soldier, and will remain a soldier to my dying day."

"Richtofen, you're going too far—"

"I don't give a damn what happens to your plans, your next war, your scheming, and your politics. I have thirty men fighting for their lives, fighting for sheer survival, and I am not going to listen to any more of your *shit*."

As he turned toward the door, General von Hoeppner shouted at him and he halted. "I made you! I picked you up when you were about to be court-martialed and gave you this squadron! Now I can only hope the British—"

Richtofen threw back his head and barked a short bitter laugh. "Never doubt it, General. They will."

Anthony Fokker put his face in his hands and muttered, "What are we coming to!"

Richtofen stalked out of the room and slammed the door behind him.

There was one man waiting in the outer office: Hermann Goering. He sat in a straight-backed chair and looked up at the raging Richtofen, and his pudgy face was innocent-looking. But Richtofen knew he had overheard every word that had been spoken inside the messhall.

Richtofen paused for a moment, his face still curdled with contempt, gazing down at Goering.

"Your turn now," he said at last, and stalked down the hallway.

Rain tapped lightly on the tin room of the wardroom shack and, looking out the window, Roy Brown saw that the long night was coming to an end. From what little light there was in the east, he could tell it was going to be a gray and bleak day. Brown was sitting at a table, sipping warm milk from a cup. He had been sitting there a long time. This was his third cup of warm milk. He looked ill and tired, and near the edge of collapse.

The door opened and Wop May stomped in and snapped on the light. Brown flinched, and squinted his eyes.

"Roy!"

"Morning, Wop."

"What the hell are you sitting in here for, all by yourself?"

Brown reached down and patted his stomach and made a rueful face, and May understood at once that his friend's ulcers were acting up again.

"Is it time?" asked Brown.

"It's time."

He rose slowly. "I'm ready. Let's get going."

Wop May clapped him on the shoulder as they headed toward the door. "Buck up, old man. It's almost over. Probably before the leaves fall again we'll be—"

"It'll never be over," said Brown quietly. "One day they'll change the system of dating. *B.C.* will mean *before combat*. *A.D.* will mean *after death*."

"Come off it, Roy! They can't kill us all."

They were outside now. The dawn was chill and the drizzle made them hunch up their shoulders as they plodded across the grass toward the flight line.

"They don't need to kill us all," said Brown, giving way to his profound war-weariness. "We're already dead."

And May couldn't think of anything to say to that.

Behind them, in the empty wardroom, a fly-specked calendar on the wall announced that it was April 21st, 1918. Only God Himself knew that it was to be the day Baron Manfred von Richtofen would die.

Chapter 15

Richtofen was nearly ready.

In his incredible junk-shop of a room, with fragments of planes he had downed covering three of the four walls, he was having a last cup of coffee with his brother. Lothar was touched to have been invited in. It had been several weeks since Manfred had acted like the warm, friendly brother he used to know.

"Read me that letter, will you, Lothar, while I finish dressing?"

"You need a secretary, don't you—all that mail from admirers."

"This one's from Funck. I've been expecting a package."

While Richtofen pulled on his flying suit, Lothar picked up the letter and read: "Esteemed Herr Rittmeister. Because of war shortages, we beg to inform that the silver required to make your trophy cups is no longer available. We can, however, supply an identical cup made up in base-metal plated with tin, the same being most attractive."

"I should have gone after that boar, little brother."

Lothar glanced over at him and saw the faraway look in Manfred's eyes. "I beg your pardon?"

"Never mind," Manfred said gruffly, coming back into the grim present again. "I'll have to write Funck and tell him I don't want the tin cups." He buttoned the top button under his chin and smiled humorlessly at his brother. Then he took a look at himself in the big mirror.

Lothar thought this might be a good time to ask a question that had been on his mind since the night before. "What went on at Hoeppner's meeting, Manfred? Everyone walked out of there looking as if they had personally lost the war."

"It was nothing, little brother. Just routine. Let's get going."

Disappointed, Lothar went through the door his brother held open for him.

Before closing it, Manfred took one last look inside and held his gaze steady for a moment, hoping against hope he would not see what he most feared.

But there it was—gradually superimposing itself over the objects in the room there came a second image. And then it was gone. He closed the door.

It was cold and rainy outside as the two men joined the other pilots heading across the field toward their planes.

"Now I know what pheasants feel like in the autumn," grumbled one pilot.

"Did they promise you a comfortable war when you enlisted?" asked another.

"Enlist hell—they drafted me."

"Drafted?" inquired a third pilot. "I didn't know they drafted men into the Flying Service."

"They've just begun," said Ernst Udet. And he directed a question at the first pilot. "Do you have any specific complaint?"

"Me?" said the man, somewhat defensively. "Not really. I just wish we could paint these planes a nice drab brown. The English can see us coming five miles away."

The pilots began to peel off for their individual planes now. Max Holzapfel was beside the Triplane, busy screwing a panel back into place just behind the engine.

"Good morning, Herr Rittmeister."

Richtofen stood looking at the blood-red machine. He shook his head. "Sometimes I feel as if I've been married to this machine forever."

Holzapfel wiped his hands on a rag and looked at his leader with concern. "I think," he said softly, hesitantly, "it will be over soon, Herr Rittmeister."

The words had an ominous sound to Richtofen, and he glared at the crewman.

"The war, sir. I mean the war."

"Of course."

Now Lothar called out from the cockpit of the next plane: "Hey, Manfred. Look at Goering. Isn't he joining us today?"

Richtofen looked around and saw the stocky officer standing at the edge of the flying field, his hands clasped behind him, watching the flight preparations.

"He's been grounded," said Richtofen, smiling sardonically. "By order of General von Hoeppner."

"Grounded? Well, isn't that odd . . ."

"Not really," said Richtofen. Turning to Holzapfel now, he barked a brusque command: "Start the engine!"

"Yes, Herr Rittmeister!"

Moments later Richtofen was airborne, heading into his last battle, heading toward that immortality all true warriors seek.

It was just past 7 A.M. when the two formations caught sight of each other. Wop May saw the blood-red Triplane suddenly emerge out of a cloud bank, followed by the tightly massed squadron. The Canadian immediately kicked his Camel into a slanted dive toward the German ace of aces, his heart pounding violently with the surge of excitement he felt.

Richtofen slipped away from the rigidly diving Camel, moving the maneuverable Fokker out of the way with a minimum of adjustment, then turned in toward one of the British planes on the flank. Richtofen had fallen in love with the DR-1, for its grace and power and speed, and now once again he easily brought the beautiful machine into a position of attack behind the British plane. The bullets from his initial burst smashed the Spad's undercarriage and drilled through the fuselage, and the plane wobbled and drifted into a helpless side-slip. Richtofen knew that he had his eightieth victory.

As he paused to watch the plane head into a steep doomed dive, a sudden burst of tracer fire snapped him back to alertness and he swiveled his head around to see who was on his tail. He smiled to himself. It was the same Englishman who had dived on him a minute or two before.

With a minimum of effort Richtofen looped upward and went into a hanging stall and then—just as May zoomed by below—dropped down onto his tail and squeezed off a burst.

May, stunned with fear, jammed his plane into a steep dive, glanced over his shoulder and found to his dismay that the blood-red Triplane was right behind him. He pulled out of the dive dangerously close to the ground, and Richtofen was still there, close on his tail.

It was at this point that Roy Brown saw them and, recognizing the Fokker, knew that his Canadian comrade was in the worst trouble of his life. The two were out of the main battle area, heading due south, close to the ground, just skimming and hedge-hopping above the trenches and lunar landscape below. Brown, at one edge of the main dogfight zone himself, was in a good position to intercept. With a kick of the rudder, he banked into a curving dive that would bring him within range of the Triplane—he hoped.

Meanwhile Wop May felt exactly like a trapped animal, as the Triplane came so close behind him that it almost nudged him. For one moment he thought Richtofen intended to chew the Camel's tail off with his propeller.

For Richtofen was not firing, although he had been in perfect position for several seconds.

And Roy Brown, his face frozen with tension, urged his plane on, cursing it, hunching his body forward jerkily as though to make it move faster. Slowly, too slowly, he was catching up. In a few seconds he would be within shooting range.

And still Richtofen did not fire on Wop May.

About a mile down-range, a grizzled Australian anti-aircraft gunner sat watching the three planes approach. He figured them for British planes all, probably heading back to their base. But he kept his eye on them just the same, for he had never seen a three-plane formation quite like this one. Idly he fingered the heavy button-control of his Bofors gun and waited.

Three hundred yards away, also down-range from the oncoming planes but in the zone of an adjoining Canadian regiment, a young Canadian sergeant was also watching the three planes, noticing how the last plane in line was creeping up on the other two. Not sure what was happening, he nevertheless reached for his heavy Lewis gun and propped it atop an ammunition crate on the edge of the trench. And waited.

A few seconds later both men, the Australian and the Canadian, recognized the situation for what it was. The Aussie swung his long barrel toward the blood-red plane and squinted through the sights, and zeroed in. The young Canadian pressed his cheek into the stock of the Lewis gun, inserted his right index finger into the trigger-guard, and zeroed in.

But still Richtofen did not fire. And the reason he did not fire was because his mind, as well as his eyes, were playing tricks on him. He saw the Sopwith Camel up ahead with its pilot turning frantically around in the cockpit to stare at him in an agony of terror. But there were two Sopwiths and there were two pilots, and as if that was not enough, the pilot's face was the face of

Lanoe Hawker. He knew that if he squeezed the trigger that the Englishman's head would turn to bloody jelly and come flowing back all over him and drench him in blood and bits of flesh. And the prospective hideousness of that was too much for him.

Behind him, Roy Brown decided he had come just into possible range—although it was going to be a long distance for the bullets to travel—and he squeezed the trigger . . .

While below him, to one side, the grizzled Australian anti-aircraft gunner hammered the heavy buttoncontrol of the Bofors . . .

While below him, off to the other side, the young Canadian sergeant held his breath and slowly squeezed the trigger of the Lewis gun as he swung it into convergence with the blood-red plane rushing past . . .

And the three lines of tracers came together in perfect unison.

Richtofen sat back against the seat, his eyes closed. The debris from the converging tracers blew past him into the slipstream, but he kept his eyes closed. The Fokker, no longer beautiful, began to wobble and falter in the air. And Richtofen, no longer graceful, no longer handsome, forced his eyes open and forced his hands back onto the control column. As his life's blood poured out of him he somehow brought the controlling surfaces into a precarious kind of balance and guided the plane gently downward toward a flat stretch of the battlefield ahead. For even though the pain was intense and growing worse, Richtofen's final wish was to die in control of his plane.

And that wish was granted.

Two minutes later, just after the last of the swirling dust settled around the immobile plane, a sweating Australian soldier came jogging up to the plane and took a quick look over the side of the cockpit.

"My God," he muttered. "It's—we've shot down the bloody baron himself."

And when Roy Brown landed his Camel at the British aerodrome and switched off the engine and started to climb down, he saw men from all directions running toward him.

"Ambushed the baron, did you!" yelled Fred Thompson.

"You're the best bloody killer of them *all*," shouted Gerald Murphy.

And Wop May ran up and yelled, "You were right, Roy. You were always right!"

Brown stood looking down into their wildly exultant faces, and they all seemed bestial and swollen with bloodlust; and he was sick in his heart.

"Leave me alone," he murmured, stepping down and moving into the crowd of pilots and crewmen and staff people. But no one heard him. Those who saw his face only thought his ulcers were acting up.

Thirty miles to the east, Max Holzapfel stood waiting in the rain, hugging his arms around himself against the chill, scanning the horizon to the west, looking for a lost plane that would never return.

Chapter 16

Another time, another place . . .

Max Holzapfel stood puffing his pipe and watching the young boy asleep in the gently swaying replica of the plane that had never returned.

The boisterous meeting in the beer hall across the square was coming to an end, amid waves of martial shouting. Holzapfel reached out and softly shook the boy's shoulder as he sat slumped in the little cockpit.

"Willi . . . Willi, wake up. It's time to wake up. Your father will be coming soon."

The boy awoke with a start, sat up, and glared at the older man.

"I am not *Willi*," he announced sullenly. "I am Herr Wilhelm Alfried Kulppner, and my father is an important man in the Party."

Just then a wild explosion of applause and hurrahs sounded from across the way; the doors of the beer hall were flung open and men began coming out. The first two emerged together, side-by-side. The one on the left was tall and fat, and walked with a ridiculously arrogant strut. The one on the right was ordinary looking except for the square dark mustache and the way his

dark hair fell across his forehead. Both men acknowl-
edged the wild cheers with the stiff, right-handed Nazi
salute, and then climbed into a waiting Mercedes. No
one in the crowd had to be told they were Goering and
the Fuhrer himself.

The Mercedes drove off and the crowd began to
disperse. Willi's father appeared, and Holzapfel helped
the sleepy boy down to the ground. The Brownshirt
tipped Holzapfel, nodded curtly, and walked away with
his son.

"When you are grown, Willi," Holzapfel heard him
say, "they will give you a fine plane of your *own* to
fly."

The boy was instantly excited. "Really, Poppa? Like
that one back there?"

"Oh, no, Willi—much finer, much faster . . ."

And as they disappeared around the corner into the
darkness, Holzapfel wondered when it would all end.

War in Tandem editions

Westerns in Tandem editions

Ambush at Antlers Spring   Will Cook 17½p

Rio Chama   Bennett Garland 17½p

Gunlock   Sam Bowie 17½p

The Wild Bunch   Brian Fox 25p

A Dollar to Die For   Brian Fox 20p

For a Few Dollars More   Joe Millard 20p

The Good, The Bad and The Ugly   Joe Millard 20p

The Good Guys and the Bad Guys   Joe Millard 25p

Valdez is Coming   Elmore Leonard 25p

The Moonshine War   Elmore Leonard 25p

The McMasters   Dean Owen 25p

Lawman   Grant Freeling 25p

Sabata   Brian Fox 25p

Macho Callahan   Joe Millard 25p

U-F.O.s in Tandem editions

New U.F.O. Breakthrough (Allende Letters)   Brad Steiger
   & Joan Whritenour 17½p

Flying Saucers from Outer Space   Donald E. Keyhoe   ..   30p

Flying Saucers are Hostile   Brad Steiger & Joan Whritenour   25p

Strangers from the Skies   Brad Steiger 25p

The Sky People   Brinsley Le Poer Trench 25p

Science Fiction in Tandem editions

The Paw of God Rex Gordon 17½p
> When happiness became as much a threat to Man as atomic warfare

Invaders of Space Murray Leinster 17½p
> An obsolescent space-ship on a life-or-death mission

Operation Terror Murray Leinster 17½p
> Mankind faces extinction at the hands of interplanetary visitors

Shield Poul Anderson 20p
> The device gave total immunity to weapons – but who would gain possession of it?

Planet of No Return Poul Anderson 25p
> Man must search for colonies beyond the stars, but can he find a permanent home there?

The Time-Hoppers Robert Silverberg 25p
> Every human need was fulfilled in the 25th century, yet they still yearned to escape

Hawksbill Station Robert Silverberg 25p
> Banished from the complicated world of the far future to the barren emptiness of the remote past

The Man in the Maze Robert Silverberg 25p
> Solitary and embittered, hiding from the loathing of his fellows, he must be lured out of his refuge to save the world

Light a Last Candle Vincent King 25p
> 'Vivid stuff, a tale of internecine strife between mutated and modified people in the far future'. *Edmund Cooper, Sunday Times*

Name.. ....

Address.. ....

Titles required ....

....

....

....

....

....

....

....